Frozen Time

Studies in Austrian Literature, Culture and
Thought

Translation Series

General Editors:

Jorun B. Johns
Richard H. Lawson

Anna Kim

Frozen Time

Translated and with an
Introduction by
Michael Mitchell

Ariadne Press
Riverside, California

Ariadne Press would like to express its appreciation to the
Bundesministerium für Unterricht, Kunst und Kultur, Vienna for
assistance in publishing this book.

.KUNST

Translated from the German
Die gefrorene Zeit
© Literaturverlag Droschl, Graz-Wien 2008

Library of Congress Cataloging-in-Publication Data

Kim, Anna, 1977-
 [Gefrorene Zeit. English]
 Frozen time / Anna Kim ; translated [from the German] by
Michael Mitchell.
  p. cm. -- (Studies in Austrian literature, culture and thought.
Translation series)
 Originally published in German as Die gefrorene Zeit.
 ISBN 978-1-57241-172-2 (alk. paper)
 1. Albanians--Kosovo (Republic)--Fiction. 2. Albanians--Austria—
Fiction. 3. Kosovo War, 1998-1999--Psychological aspects--Fiction.
4. Kosovo War, 1998-1999--Social aspects--Fiction. 5. Disappeared
persons' families--Fiction. 6. War victims--Fiction.
I. Mitchell, Michael, 1941- II. Title.
PT2711.I5G4413 2010
833'.92--dc22   2010013632

Cover Design
Designer: Beth A. Steffel

Introduction

Anna Kim was born in Daejeon, South Korea, in 1977. When she was still an infant, her family moved to Germany, where her father, an artist, became a visiting professor in Braunschweig. After a period in Giessen, the family moved to Vienna in 1984, where she grew up and still lives. She was brought up bilingually but regards German as her mother tongue "even though it is not the tongue of my mother," her Korean is "only good enough for simple conversations" and she does not write in Korean, only in German.

She studied philosophy and theater studies in Vienna, finishing with a master's thesis on Georg Lukács's *Theory of the Novel*. She has published short stories, poems and essays in magazines and anthologies; her first novel, *Die Bilderspur* (Trail of Pictures), appeared in 2004 and a volume of poems, *das sinken ein bückflug* (sinking a stooping flight) in 2006. She has received numerous awards and prizes; *Frozen Time* was awarded the 2009 Heinrich Treichl Humanity Prize of the Austrian Red Cross.

The conflict between Albanians and Serbs in Kosovo, a region of the former Yugoslavia, a conflict that goes back to the Middle Ages, forms the background to *Frozen Time*, but the novel is not *about* the conflict. It focuses on an individual, an Albanian whose wife is one of the hundreds of thousands of people who went missing during the conflict. She was probably abducted by a Serbian paramilitary organization, Arkan's Tigers, largely made up of criminals, but that is merely one detail in the "case" of her disappearance; what the novel concentrates on is the husband, his grief, his sense of loss and his insistence that his wife is missing, not dead. The narrator is a woman working for the Red Cross tracing service who gradually becomes personally involved with him.

1

This focus enables Kim to explore themes of general human interest, in particular the question of identity (does a dead person have identity? for example), rather than a specific sociopolitical situation.

There is a wide range of language used – the standardized questions of the Red Cross interview, the sober prose of official reports of atrocities, descriptions of Albanian folk tales and customs, of life in Kosovo – but most of it is marked by the personal tone of the narrator whose account focuses on and is addressed to the central character: "you did this, you said that, you felt that...." One touch is impossible to render in English: the initial tracing service interview is conducted with the formal "you," i.e., "*Sie*," while the rest of the book, including the opening section before going back in time to the first interview, uses the informal "*du*" deriving from their close personal relationship.

A further feature of the style is a striking and often personal use of imagery. Images are sometimes inserted abruptly, without the relevance being elaborated, for example: "Nusha sighs in protest, gives a little wail, <u>no vise</u>, the sound climbs out of her mouth of its own free will," when I asked the author about "no vise," she replied, "Yes, that's what I meant, that Nusha doesn't suppress the sigh by force," in other cases, she said that she used a word "precisely because it was unusual" or had personal associations or that she liked it because it "has such a range of meaning." Such choices, together with word play, are even more widespread in her poems; in *Frozen Time*, the reader needs to accept the *force* of the images rather than trying to spell out the precise *meaning* of each. It is one of the features that makes this short novel such a powerful evocation of what is meant by being human, by humanity.

Michael Mitchell

Translator's Note:

The following Albanian words are used in the text without explanation:
ambeltore = confectioner's, sweet shop
çaj = tea
hoxha = Muslim priest
Kanun = Law
Kina = China
Nënë Therese = Mother Theresa
quebaptore = coffee roaster
Rruga = street

Acronyms:

KFOR = NATO forces in Kosovo
OSCE = Organization for Security and Cooperation in Europe
UÇK = Kosovo Liberation Army
UNHCR = United Nations High Commission for Refugees
UNMIK = United Nations Interim Mission in Kosovo

The Albanian spelling has been used for all place names; exceptions are "Kosovo" and "Pristina" for which either the Albanian (Kosova, Prishtinë) or the anglicized form (Kosovo, Pristina) was used, depending on perspective.

It is strange how the dead leap out on us at street corners, or in dreams.

Virginia Woolf, *The Waves*

"Ante mortem data (AMD) is comprehensive information given by the person who last saw the missing person and knows the circumstances under which they disappeared, or by a person who knew him/her well. AMD is collected to assist with the possible identification of human remains. The questionnaire used during the interview asks for detailed information regarding clothing, physical characteristics, medical and dental traits, as well as personal effects carried by the person at the time of disappearance.

The International Committee of the Red Cross and the National Societies involved have almost completed the collection of AMD in countries of the former Yugoslavia and, together with the International Tracing Network of the Red Cross, will now begin collecting AMD from the families of the missing living outside countries of the Former Yugoslavia."

AMD *Collection Communications Guide*, August 2004

1

Your voice, slight, falls close to my ear, as if you were standing beside me and in a whisper you say, thinking more than speaking, *they've finally found her* —
my fodder: memory, dowry and touchstone. Does that mean that *it* cannot be communicated piecemeal? And yet I am ready to discover the impotence of language and give in, going over your words little by little and becoming like you: vulnerable. Impossible to describe this beforehand, the meaning will appear afterwards, after the withdrawal.
You repeat, they've finally found her. I ask, how do you feel?
Bad, you say, bad, not the least bit relieved. Now at last you know, I say, you wanted to know. My encouragement drops into a void; I could have caught it, had I meant what I said. You remain silent. I'm very sorry, I say; you interrupt, would you go with me, you ask, would you accompany me to Prishtinë, I don't feel like going there by myself.

Six months earlier: I wouldn't have met you if I'd handed the case over to a much more experienced, more professional colleague, so I worked my way through the questions, ignoring the feeling that I was intruding on your diary, on those pages I would pass over if I had the choice; in my head the instruction: *steer clear of their grief*
— don't respond to it, never respond. Avoid feelings, look for facts: names, figures, places. As far as possible no interruptions, lock doors, secure rooms, switch off telephones. Don't risk a confrontation, explain the situation, point out that it takes time to analyze the data, the identification process takes a long time, longer than is good. There were problems in the past, not enough care was taken, graves were opened and filled in again, that won't happen

7

again. Don't forget — the interviews are given voluntarily. If he refuses to answer a question, don't insist, leave a visiting card, ask for an answer when he feels up to it. If he can't remember certain particulars, ask supplementary questions to prompt his memory. Repeat questions, reformulate and repeat them at a later date, details will emerge, too important to remain forgotten.

February, early afternoon, sunny, cold, bright, spring is in the air already. I drive to Paulanergasse and park outside the annex of the Vienna Red Cross, a white cube with frosted-glass windows, non-see-through, two plastic tables with garden chairs in the lobby, a wooden coatstand, cork bulletin boards; behind the curtains is the rest of the family, a raincoat and a bicycle.

First door on the right down the corridor, the interview room, completely white, the floor a touch darker perhaps, a pale birchwood table, chairs with rubber tips on the bottom of legs which refuse to slide, they have to be lifted up every time; on the wall right next to the door a whiteboard with colored magnets and felttips, at the farther end of the room an abandoned computer. On the table a bottle of water, three glasses, a carton of orange juice and a plate of biscuits which will remain untouched the whole afternoon; after the interview I will dispose of them, throw them one by one into the trash.

You're twenty minutes late, you say that you did try to open the door to the building, but it was locked, so you walked up and down the street keeping a lookout for me, Nora. You stand in the doorway, uncertain what to do, hands in your pockets; I would have said you were around forty, find out later that you're twenty-nine. I invite you into the interview room, seat you with your back to the window, sit on your right, hiding behind the map of Kosovo, a chart with color

8

samples, a measuring tape, handkerchiefs, ballpoints, and a pile of blank sheets of paper. Experience has taught me to be at least partially invisible, that way all of you who are sick speak more freely –

last week Azra, straight, dark-brown hair with a reddish tinge, hollow cheeks. She suspects, she feels, she is certain that her husband is buried in the mass grave outside Z., a village on the Serbian border. She says she knows, she knows for sure, I ask how she can be so certain, she says it's a gnawing feeling, quietly gnawing away at her, stemming from her desire to know whether she can finally mourn and feel relief, but there's no relief, Azra says, as long as hope remains that he may still be alive. Playing with her wedding ring, she says she's now been married exactly the same length of time as she's been looking for him, a ray of light catches the slim band of gold, casting flashes on the wall. No memories anymore, she says, all the images have been lost, they slipped out of my eyes one after the other and crept along my eyelids into a blind spot.

You haven't spoken yet, you close your eyes for a moment; your voice carefully combs the silence, finally settling on the words, *I am looking for my wife, I have been looking for seven years.*

What is your name?
You hand me your passport.
Luan Alushi.
The missing woman is your wife?
You nod, I note down the time and place of the interview: Vienna, 5 February 2005.
When did your wife disappear? If you don't know the precise date, indicate a period of time, please.
You leaf through a small, thick address book, it fits perfectly in your hand, the pages tattered, gold-edged, bound in crocodile leather, the binding brown to dark brown, brown

because it's been much used?

On 23 December 1998.

When did you last speak to her?

The day before, 22 December, a few hours before she was arrested.

When was the last time you saw your wife?

You shake your head.

I can't remember, either in October or November, during the holiday, All Saints' Day, All Souls' Day.

Where did you last see her?

In my village, B., in Kosova, about sixty kilometers to the north of Prishtinë.

Why was there this gap between the last time you saw her and the last time you spoke to her?

At the time I was working in Vienna, at a hotdog stand and on building sites, I spent my holidays, including public holidays, with my family in B.

Traveling back and forward then, now settled in Vienna. Later I discover that you started working in Austria when you were sixteen in order to support your family.

War broke out a few months later, on 24 March 1999.

You cough, jiggle your feet. You breathe out audibly, concealing a sigh.

On that day I set off as early as possible.

On which day?

23 December. On 23 December I set off at four in the morning. The streets were empty. It only took nine hours. Nine hours isn't much.

Again your eyes go from me to the door. You clear your throat, stroke the table top, screw up your eyes, attempt a smile, unsuccessfully.

I missed her by three hours. Three hours.

Then your voice fails, you have to clear your throat to get it back. You don't look at me while you speak, press your lips

together, clear your throat, again and again.
What do you mean, you missed her?
You sigh, turn around, head facing the window.
Who was the last person to see her alive?
For a moment everything is quiet, apart from the distant roar, the afternoon traffic.
My family. My mother, my brother, his wife and four children.

You agreed to answer the questionnaire, but sometimes your hands tremble, tremble in concert, as do your words, an aftershock in your throat; you stare at the door, as if it were a window with an unforgettable landscape in it, then wake, rummage in your pocket and place your wife's passport, a slim photograph album and your marriage certificate on the table. The Antemortem Questionnaire: twenty-two sections recording the distinguishing features of a missing person, characteristics that person possessed while still alive, *ante mortem*, with the aim, through the *post mortem* analysis and comparison of skeletons, pieces of bone, data, of finding them. What we find is not the person, but their remains, their innermost essence, if you like; on the other hand, what is left, the last remaining scraps, are mere externals and yet they — the bereaved and the researchers — talk of identity, meaning *complete identity with*, at the same time *inner unity of the person*. The levels intermingle, seem inseparable: it is unavoidable — the corpse becomes an individual. How long can this thought last? Only as long as the human fragment has not been seen, as long as its death can remain an abstraction, an idea.
The deceased don't care whether their identity is found or not, for them it doesn't matter whether they have one or whether it was lost over the last few years. From their point of view, it only exists for others, not for themselves. If it is eventually found, it is physical and coincidental, coincidental because it is never really a matter of their identity, but solely

of its classification.

Identity according to the questionnaire is clearly defined, it consists of sex, age, illnesses, clothing, eyewitness reports and chance encounters. Our conversations are an attempt to home in on the missing person, to tie them down, hold on to them. Perhaps it is true that the uniqueness of a person — their identity? — does in fact not die with them but can be found long after their death. Every sentence is an *act*, every word is *utilized*: to establish identity by speaking, by putting it into words, eats away at its substance since the person is replaced by talk, following in unknown footsteps that are always several sizes too big; in addition the alien perspective is alienating —

and one particular distinguishing feature steals the show: being missing mutates into the birthmark on their forehead, into the scar on their cheek, into their predilection for swimming in the rain, strolling along streets after midnight.

Who told you about the abduction?

My mother, Emine Alushi.

Your voice clouds over, a little; your eyes are glassy around the edges, you're constantly kneading your hands.

Even before I got there I could tell something had happened. The front door was wide open, our neighbors and my brother were out in the street, without jackets even though it was very cold.

Extra thick gloves, the gardens on the way into the village covered in snow, your breath leaving traces in the air. When you see the commotion, you accelerate, park at the bottom of the drive, run the last few yards to the door, your brother Fehmi's waving to you, Emine's screaming, *they've arrested her, they've taken her away!* everyone's talking at once, you're faced with incessant tears, you ask them to be quiet, who have they taken, you ask, who? *your wife!* they wail, you try to calm them down, it must be a mistake, a misunderstanding, why should they arrest her? you say, you want them to tell you everything, right from the beginning, Emine screams, *three hours ago, they came three hours ago and took her and Ali away!* I interrupt.

Who is Ali?

My neighbor.

You sigh, I've disturbed your rhythm. I give you a glass of water, you take a drink, beads of sweat on your forehead, your knees twitching.

What happened?

A dozen masked men at the door, hammering furiously, speaking Albanian, some in uniform, some in civilian clothes, a few wearing black vests and red gloves, most of them masked, only one isn't, with long, blond hair. They order them to open the door, the family's uncertain what to do, flee or hide, Emine wants to talk to the men, but Fehmi and his sons have to disappear first, she's heard of arrests, but they're only after men. Fehmi, she orders, you all go and hide in the cellar, only after that will we open the door and then only a crack. The men push her into the living room, bawling that they want *weapons, gold and money!* the women don't reply and they hit them with their rifles, making the children whimper. We haven't got anything, Emine cries, her upper body black and blue from the blows, they break her hand, we haven't got any weapons, *Bullshit!* They don't believe her, kick her, slap her across the face, chain the children to each other by the neck, force them to kneel on the kitchen floor, your wife's insulted, taken away, no one dares speak out, *bad things brood in their ears.* They hear the vehicle door open and close, the engine start.

Did anyone see the vehicle?

My nephew, he said it was a white VW minibus, the tire tracks could still be seen the next morning.

How were the men's faces covered?

13

Black scarves over their mouths and noses.

What were the uniforms like? Did your family notice any particular emblems?

They were green, the badges had a white eagle.

I've heard about them, the *White Eagles* and *Arkan's Tigers*, paramilitary units who hoped to earn more than fifteen thousand dollars a month from the war, not counting the bonuses for villages destroyed, expulsions carried out, whole regions cleared, their *speciality*, and finally taking individual refugees hostage and only returning them to their families for large sums of money, provided the hostage survived —

We suspect the same thing, but we say nothing.

Only at this point do I have to ask the name of the missing woman: the questions strictly according to the schedule, diverging from it impossible. The past tense to be avoided, at all costs.

What is your wife called?

Fahrie Alushi.

Does she have a nickname?

No.

What was her maiden name?

Ivanova.

Where was she born?

Prishtinë.

When was she born?

5 August 1977.

Do you have any personal papers of your wife's in your possession, apart from her passport?

No.

Do you have any photos of your wife?

You place color photocopies of the passport on the table: the background is turquoise blue, Fahrie is wearing a grey suit, black bangs hang down over her forehead.

Where did she live before the war?
In B.
What was her profession?
Student.
Have you ever heard from people outside your family that your wife did not survive?
You stare at me, as if you don't understand, how could you? you think your wife's still alive, or do you have your doubts? I'd prefer not to ask the question either, I'd prefer to skip this part, believe me, but still —
I go on; I notice that my voice becomes softer, you frown, as if you were trying to bring your ears close to me.
If so, did the witness make a written statement? Do you know where this statement might be? Do you know in what area the body might be buried, according to the witness?
Are you indignant? Are you horrified? I can't tell, your look holds me back, a wall; you fold your arms.
No, there is no such witness, but I'm sure there's a list of all the graves, hidden away somewhere, buried —
just as there's a *Book of Sightings?* A list describing which of the missing persons have been seen, where and when; it's said to go around the restaurants and cafés, a book that promises miracles, but it appears at arbitrary moments, just as arbitrary as the abductions, arrests that are its subject.

What was your wife wearing when she was abducted? Trousers or skirt? Was she barefoot or wearing shoes? If shoes, what kind?
You leaf through your address book.
She was wearing a long, black cotton dress, pantyhose, boots and a white blouse.
Was she wearing underwear?
You nod.
What exactly? Bra and undershirt? Panties?

15

A shake of the head, you haven't noted it down. When you reply, I suspect you're only doing it to fill in the form.

A white cotton undershirt and white panties.

What color were the boots and pantyhose? What were the shoes and stockings made of?

The boots were brown leather, the pantyhose —

you shrug your shoulders, you don't know, and the less you know, the more unlikely it seems to you that you will ever see Fahrie again, the more you feel guilty, as if it were in your power to bring her, with each question you manage to answer, one step more away from her presumed imprisonment.

What brand were her clothes? Can you remember where your wife liked to shop, in which store?

A helpless look.

Was she wearing anything apart from underwear beneath her blouse, a T-shirt perhaps?

No.

What was the blouse like? Did it have short or long sleeves, puffed sleeves? Did it have a particular pattern? Was it frilled or fitted at the waist?

You sigh, flick through the photos in the album. No white blouse.

I don't know, I can't remember, striped perhaps, yes, I think it was striped.

What color were the stripes? Were they narrow, broad or patterned?

The evening darkens thoughts, you know this trail, it's the way a tricky path behaves. Now it's back, your sigh, what is it, the prelude to tears? At least you sigh several times before you start to cry, and sometimes your sighing seems to replace crying until it becomes irreplaceable.

How tall is your wife?

She was small, delicate —

you show me, draw her body with your hands, stop abruptly.

You sigh, a suppressed, almost inaudible sigh, but still. You indicate that there are no suitable words left, at the same time you search, hands clutching thin air, for the right expressions. The pause remains because it's a blank. As long as there are no *true words*, that box must remain empty —
She's small, a head shorter than me.
About one meter sixty?
Yes.
Or is sighing just a sound after all, catapulted out from inside and then, like a boomerang, back in from outside? A personal, unjustifiable physical expression, also unjustifiable in the sense of unanswerable, or what could be the right response to sighing? There seems to be no word to match the potency of a sigh, all comfort loses power, shrinks the moment one expresses it; all at once the words, light as a feather, disappear shamefacedly in the conversation that is no conversation. It's impossible to answer the other's sighs with a sigh, not mocking, aping, but with a sympathetic, powerfully expressive sigh, full of significance, pregnant with meaning, but still months away from giving birth.
What color is her hair?
Dark brown, almost black, tight ringlets.
Long or short?
Shoulder length, wet it's longer than dry.
But perhaps sighing is a metaphor for grief, a metaphor for the act of crying, related to real crying in the way the idea is to reality; basically sighing gets one nowhere, but as a symbol it creates a substitute: an image, an imagining, a symbol of a state of mind, a metaphor for tears.
Does she have any gray hair?
No.
Does she dye it?
No.
Or there are two tongues living inside you, a past and a

17

present one feeding off two different memories, identities. The split is articulated in fractured language, hybrid sentences: in your sighing. So your attempt not to lose contact with that lost language, by constantly making excursions to today, results in a mishmash. The translations are futile: clearly your speech has anchored itself at the *end of language*.

Does she write with the right or the left hand? Or is she ambidextrous?

She's right-handed.

Does she wear spectacles? If she does, can you describe the frames?

No. She has very good eyesight.

Does she have any scars on her body, from an operation or a wound, or does she have a tattoo, a particularly striking birthmark?

She has a scar on her thigh. The skin's darker, a large, round, brown mark.

Does she take any regular medication?

No.

Does she have diabetes? Does she suffer from asthma?

No.

Perhaps your sighing points to the previously existent, now lost answers. *Once upon a time, long, long ago* there were answers, more than one to every question, comfortable in their doll nest, *catalog*, taking the cozy warmth for granted. Now you think there's only one possible answer to everything, all that remains are the pauses between your sentences.

Has she ever had an operation? Has she had an operation on her head, her brain?

No.

Did she ever break any limbs, arms, legs?

No.

Does she have a limp?

No.

Does she have any prostheses, artificial limbs?

No.

This explanation is too innocuous, much too innocuous. The fact is, you've forgotten the rules of speaking, you've forgotten what it's like to understand and to be understood. Your sighs always express the same answer because that's the only one left. After endless days and nights spent going over things in your mind, you are *drained of understanding* to the limit.

Is she a smoker or a nonsmoker?

She doesn't smoke.

Was she pregnant when she was abducted?

Short pause.

No.

Does she have any fillings in her teeth?

You nod, I show you a diagram of a set of teeth, ask you to mark the fillings, you hesitate, you'd rather not say, you might get it wrong.

Had she had any teeth pulled?

A wisdom tooth, top right.

Does she have any gold teeth, silver teeth, broken teeth, crowns, black teeth?

You shake your head.

Is there a gap between her middle two top-front teeth? Is there a gap between her middle two bottom-front teeth?

Again a shake of the head.

After all, if you consider the nature of a sigh, it could be your breath taking a rest before the next sentence, the next word, a rest on the way to meaning in the course of a mute walk on which every answer by gesture or speech has become meaningless; accordingly, your sighs would simply be a vocal expression of grief that exists outside your body but now and then slips into your eyes, nose, hands and shoulders and starts tugging away at you so that eventually, defenseless all at once,

you *break into* your body.
Does she have an overbite?
No.

The lifeless things, the so-called possessions, though without
a possessor, a home, tie the seeker to the sought one, confirm
a trail which seems immediate because it cannot be assigned
to a specific time, our sight being too dull for the under-
surface. At the same time, they are stand-ins, making
lifelessness disappear as if by magic, as if it were impossible
to belong to a dead person *in the wild*, there one just gets lost.
Did your wife have a bag with her? A little shoulder bag?
No.
A scarf or a handkerchief?
No.
The finds are not only clues but also messages, proof of the
existence of the woman who has disappeared, for which you
are desperate; it's inevitable that at some point you will
wonder whether she, Fahrie, actually existed. Doubt, like a
dog, gnaws at memory, insists on seeing, believing alone can
never be enough.
Did she have a ballpoint with her? A fountain pen or a
pencil? A notepad?
No, nothing like that.
A house key, car key, bicycle or office key?
No.
Did she have any ID with her? An identity or insurance card?
No.
The past, shaken off at a stroke, takes its revenge by
absconding from the brain. You're attached to her things, you
like remembering them, not least because for a while they
make forgetting more difficult.
Did you wife have any jewels or other valuable objects with
her?

She was wearing a necklace of yellow gold with no pendant, the necklace chain interwoven, a gold wedding ring, plain, narrow, and gold earrings in both ears.

A watch?

No.

You smile, you laugh, the idea that she might wear a watch strikes you as ridiculous. I ask you to draw the necklace, wedding ring and earrings. You need three sheets of paper, you keep making mistakes, the pencil sits awkwardly in your hand; I remember a discussion with two Bosnian sisters, one blonde, the other brunette, who were looking for their father, a fifty-two-year-old fitter who worked for a firm producing washing powder and chemicals, who always had a cotton handkerchief and a comb in his jacket pocket and had broken his femur at the beginning of the seventies, an *identifiable* injury. As they drew his belt buckle, they remarked casually that while fleeing they had seen buckets with bloody water, cut-off fingers. Their drawing turned out tiny, stuck at the top edge of the paper, underneath a turned-down corner, *as if it were trying to scramble out of the firing line.*

Did your see your wife right before she disappeared? When and by whom was she seen for the last time?

Control question, see Chapter 2, the replies must tally.

I've already told you that.

Despite that, you look in your diary for the date and time. When you give them, they agree with those you've already given us, I apologize, I say I'd made a mistake, you smile.

It doesn't matter, I've written everything down.

I put my ballpoint down, in the meantime a sunset, lamp-rise, has crept up on us; you light a cigarette.

I looked for her everywhere.

The next morning you drove to the neighboring town and asked the UÇK if they'd abducted her. You got nowhere, they said they knew nothing, nothing. You demanded to see the group commander, but you weren't allowed to speak to him, they knew nothing about a raid, nothing at all. Who else could you have asked?

In November and December 1999, I called the UNHCR, the Kosovo Red Cross, and the KFOR. They said I shouldn't call again, they would get back to me. But they gave me another number.

You tried it down there last year, at the Red Cross in Pristina, they gave you a five-figure code, you think it could be a prison number —

your mind is haunted by hordes of prisons, they spring up in sunken cellars, old laundries, dressmakers' shops, abandoned yards; I note them down. You also entered Fahrie's name in the Internet, found it on the webpage of a marriage bureau, *matrimonialbank.com*, you give me the printouts, I staple them to the form, give you a nod, of encouragement, of appreciation; then we make a list of your relatives, paternal and maternal, they are all given a number, her grandmother on her mother's side has the number 202, her grandfather on her father's side 114, her sister 204, you say that she gave blood for a DNA comparison, that was how your neighbor Ali was found, in a mass grave —

I number all the variants of family life, give them addresses and telephone numbers, thus removing the last vestiges of individuality from the form.

You say that back then you spent a long time looking for Fahrie, but you had to leave, the *war*, your mother insisted you all got out —

through *dead* mountains, bald on the summits, defiles. They look uninhabited, but that's because the houses are only too well camouflaged, they have the habit of taking cover, settling into the hillside, their roofs snowed under with leaves, twigs. You cross gorges and waterfalls, a river meandering down below, lush young greenery along the edges and toothpaste ads after the stop sign. Finally you reach the customs building, dark, zigzag tiles, next to it the entrance to the border police, a trash can and a chair outside, the light bulb on the shed, a giant pacifier gnawing at a sunshade, stone lions are sitting cross-legged at the gate beside the newspaper kiosk with no newspapers, packets of chewing gum or cigarettes, widowed, the crossing a gray steel construction with barriers, three lanes. You drive at walking pace, no room to go any faster, *laburnum* in the background; barbed wire on the ground marks a lane, going in spirals, barbed wire also as a fence, with plastic bags hanging from it in places, the backdrop an orange crane with a factory, a gray block, steel tents on the roof. Tentacles dangle from the electricity pylon, poppies bloom decorative borders.

You have five minutes to clear the house, your lunch is left untouched, not enough gas in the car for your flight, the pumps at the filling station by the hospital locked, gasoline for Albanians only at double the normal price, you decide against the narrow, twisting side streets and take the main road, a friend, *Zoran the Serb*, is guiding you, he knows which route to take to avoid the checks; you go via Fushë Kosovë to the border, manage to pass a blockade in a street, with three fingers raised.

Radio tower, makes you think of a watchtower, one window, like a Cyclops eye, a few parking spaces, a telephone booth, taxis, their yellow signs gleaming, little snack stands, tables and chairs under a light-blue awning in front of light-blue window frames, the kiosk, three bikes long, two wide, crammed in between abandoned hotdog stands; chewing-gum ads on the door, barred, covered in newspaper, you say the border districts are more conservative, normally there are almost no women out in the streets —

the compartments jam-packed, four additional trains, each

with twenty-one cars, go to Skopje every day. Those who don't make it to the railroad climb over the fences and are shot down, one after the other.

You mention that two years ago they extorted money from you, two thousand euros for a ten-minute telephone call; with whom? you asked, with your son, they said, you laughed at that, almost a happy laugh. My wife's done nothing wrong, she's innocent, she hasn't got anything to fear, you say, waiting for my reaction, I just nod, so you ask tentatively how long I've been working for the Tracing Service. For two years, I say, one year of that in Kosovo, as a trainee. You're surprised, you were in Kosova, in Prishtinë? you ask. Yes, I reply. You looked for missing persons in Kosova? Yes, I repeat, as a trainee. That's good, you say, and shake my hand.
Thank you for your help.
You stand up, go slowly to the door, but then you turn around, worried that by making this request for a search you were confirming that your wife was dead. No, I say. I try to reassure you, but you interrupt, when can you expect to hear from us? I say, that's difficult to tell but we'll make every effort, we'll be as quick as we can; you smile, you say, *of course.* Now I'm no longer afraid your voice might crack at the slightest contact with air.
As you say goodbye, you ask, shyly, when can I see you again?

2

Tomorrow I'll slip into the pale light, the quiet of the street, even before dawn, freedom, I'll say, feel in my toes. Today I'm moving the sofa, chairs and shelves around, arranging books and dishes, the herbarium with young cacti I'm going to leave on the park bench, checking every hour whether someone's going over to have a look. I'd like to wave to, shout to a young couple that the cacti are fresh, they're nowhere near dying off, the glass case will still be there in the evening, I'll take it down to the cellar, put it close to the window, sunlight will only reach the outer shoots, they'll grow until the main stem suffocates.

Later I apologize, which cheek first? I never know which cheek first, get tangled up in this form of greeting, left and right. You worked out your plan during the night, during one of those countless sleepless nights when you know you won't be able to lull yourself to sleep with thoughts and dreams since with every second the dreams will throb more urgently until you eventually become a vessel for those thoughts, a vessel that gathers the ticking of the clock, the muted barking four houses away, the distant helicopter, the irregular roar of cars and your beating heart, gathers and replays them, again and again, until the last drop of sleep trickles away.

You ask me to help you in your search for your wife, for that reason alone you carefully stuck my visiting card in your address book. You've been thinking about it for some time, you know you won't find Fahrie on your own, you need help, you know too that first of all you must arouse my sympathy, for you can't pay me.

You say, I have nightmares, night after night, and by day as well, first the feeling my eyes going numb, the air around me getting cooler, lukewarm, finally cold, then fear, it starts off small then gets bigger and bigger, makes furrows, spreads around my body, lurks in cracks and crevices so that I don't notice it when I'm trying to sweep my head clean; hours later it's back again, I can still taste it the next morning.

You say, I've stopped making plans, how could I anyway? I've no experience, making plans was Fahrie's business, you correct yourself, *is* Fahrie's business. Making plans is not possible, the future's a paradox for you just like the present, you restrict yourself to a third of the past that begins with that journey home and ends with the search for Fahrie, months later.

Correction: your present and future have been amputated, leaving traces, *phantom beings*, they complain whenever you forget your grief, even if only for a moment, your life frozen at the moment when you discovered Fahrie had disappeared, no, it's not your life that's frozen but your time, frozen time which doesn't count, you wish it would finally pass, it is passing, but as it's frozen, it passes infinitely slowly. Or is it less a matter of being frozen, more of experiencing particular minutes, days and months in an endless loop? Your awareness of everything future has faded; the here and now in which you're living is a buffer zone, a minefield, its cities ghost cities, completely *deserted of people*, but everything is in its place, covered all over with dust, otherwise unchanged, the way it was seven years ago. It's peaceful in that zone, refreshingly quiet, or is the tranquility deceptive? Only yesterday hornets were sighted, a swarm.

Frozen, you're also imprisoned, imprisoned is your expression, the *window on the soul*; the spyhole reveals a lot, reveals a man weakened by waiting, for whom it is an effort just to open one eyelid, never mind to smile. You think that to forget, to shake off knowledge, leave it behind, would be a blessing; you wish not knowing would be quicker or so slow that it's dashing on ahead of knowledge.

The present is useful. The past never stops existing, it's eternally useless. The past is the precondition for the present and everything that's perceived is already past the moment it's perceived. You say, I've never felt present, I've no choice but to be past, I *am* the past. Your present is constantly fleeing from itself, your future is inadequate. Your past refuses to have anything to do with your present; as a past it sticks to its own kind, every connection to the here and now barricades itself behind hazy images, ending up in your shake of the head, evasion, you're incapable of keeping your remembering under control, of stowing it away, a world lost in your super-memory. But your memory is gradually fading, you've been observing that for quite a while now, leaving the question: where does that leave you?

On the way home, while you're trying to persuade your memory to settle down — or, on the contrary, is it so strong that it robs itself of its own self, the dominant power enforcing oblivion? — you notice some pigeons fluttering around a piece of bread, fat pigeons cooing huskily. It attracts your attention as, with one ear on the road, you take the wrong turn. And yet memory has a direct line to immortality. (And yet the moment has a direct line to immortality.)

You want an infallible memory, one in which past and present happen simultaneously. You say: my inaccurate memories grow rampant at my expense, if they were accurate the price would be justified, you say: I want a memory packed full of relevant details, you say: it's impossible to live without memories, only with a partially functioning sand-table memory that constantly plays out the events of her departure again and again, and that's not even a proper memory since it's just something that was reported to me, but it's made such an impression on me that it produces a degree of *sleeplessness* by going over it, constantly going over it again and again. It means, you say, that I can neither remember nor forget. The forgetting you long for would above all contain the ability to cancel out memories.

You can only rid yourself of the moment which holds you captive, the moment of your return to Kosovo, if you imagine something unheard-of — automobiles with five wheels, hedgehogs on tiptoe, ghosts with sunglasses — if you dip it in black, in darkness at three in the morning. Being awake, you say, is a nightmare, sleeping switches off memories. You lie there, eyes closed, inexorably exposed to images; it's not just one moment you're compelled to analyze and interpret over and over again, it's the present and future as well; at such times you're not living in the present moment but in what has been, then you try to form the present out of elements you borrow from the past, and even in your everyday life you pretend to have *been*, you cling on to details that permit you to dismiss the present: you're saving your wages for a house that doesn't belong to you, to Fahrie and you, anymore, you note down special offers for a trip to Istanbul, Fahrie's favorite city, you glance at your watch every few hours and imagine what she *might* be doing at that moment, might be doing —
there's nothing left for it but to wait.

You say: I've given everyone my telephone number, I can always be contacted, I'm always grateful for any information or news. What you don't say is that you live off them, live through them, until doubt begins to gnaw at you and you have to discard the trail, which is no trail; what you don't say is that you couldn't exist without information or news, that your life is directly bound up with rumors, eyewitness accounts, clues.

Obsessed, lodged inside you is unbridled searching, more than a wish, wishing would be of your own free will, more than a longing, that comes nowhere near describing the extent of your need to find her; coupled with despair it is gradually consuming you, during the first few days you notice how you are turning into a brain with eyes, the rest of your body separating off, sailing away with every sentence you read, with every word that seems to bring Fahrie closer, only seems to, for the words separate you even if they promise hope, and hope is the only thing connecting you, tying you to her.

Restless, you can't sit still and read quietly, you jiggle your feet, your legs move up and down, you rock to and fro, chew your lips, your hands can't behave themselves, they don't know what they're doing, sometimes they're bobbing up and down with your legs, sometimes they're dangling at the end of your arms with no will of their own, baffled, almost astonished; searching leaves you no time for reading, you just glance over the pages, you who used to spell out, pore over every word, now you cut them off and gobble them up, a trash can for non-information, without meaning for you, your search, your mission. This practice, the content scrolling past you without revealing itself, proves its worth later; at the beginning you can't stop yourself spelling out the words, but with the letters, the words, images, scenes form which stop you getting to sleep, sleeping through, images which remind you that it's high time to find Fahrie, every minute you don't find her could mean suffering, endless suffering, even though you only note scraps of sentences; extract from a report: *200 people shot on open ground next to a school, in two trenches, 100 meters long, one meter deep, 50 centimeters wide, only buried up to the waist, heads and upper bodies remained visible for ten days, the strong stench of decay cleared the village of people,* you see, *Bosanski Novi, Bosnia,* you breathe a sigh or relief, it doesn't concern you, your eye moves on to the date, *1992*, 1992 doesn't concern you, you can hardly remember that year and you go on reading, precisely because it doesn't concern you. You waver between indifference, curiosity and sensationalism, you almost feel all this isn't real, never happened, it's something to read, that's all, you immerse yourself in the contents, moved, yes, you're moved, but then almost bored, *once again* are the words that creep in, *once again* and, click! you're away from it; then all at once you lose this distance, this brief holiday from the here and now, and tumble, collapse back into your own self, Fahrie might be among them, thirty civilians crushed by trucks, hurriedly you look for the time and place, details of women, how many? were they found? are there witnesses? and once more a sigh of relief, it was not in the vicinity of Pristina, not in your home village.

By now it's morning, you've read the whole night through, the difference between day and night in your apartment is a tightrope walk for, like you, it has gone underground in the basement; when you look out of the window, you see the grille on the sidewalk and to the right of it the underside of weeds in the asphalt. Now, after thirteen years, this room with the lace curtain with a floral pattern, the blue woolen drapes, the mini-refrigerator on the sideboard, the standard lamp of brass and yellow leather, with pipes that go up into the ceiling, hissing, gurgling, booming whenever Christel, your landlady, takes a shower, washes her hair, plates or clothes, all this is familiar, has become as much your home as the house in B. with the neighbor's rooster crowing on the dungheap next door, surrounded by puppies looking for food in the dung, their mother hasn't nearly enough milk to feed one, never mind five; and it reminds you of your niece, eight years old, whom the family said they had seen eating grass during the war, and it reminds you of the neighbor's cow, which Ali took out for a walk once a day, *she needs exercise!* and suddenly you find it hilariously funny that Vlora and Ali's cow grazed the same meadow and you can't stop laughing and topple off your chair onto the carpet, its yellowish-brown spots grass that's been torn up; you could almost have started chewing the woolen threads if you hadn't suddenly realized that in that room, three feet below ground, time no longer exists.

Fahrie's photo sails confidently into the abyss, you'd stuck it on the fridge so as never to forget her, *your wife*, already you're finding it difficult to remember how she sounded, it's the memory of her voice that disappears first of all, you say, you can still hear the sound of her body, her quiet step, the soft drag of her heels, her coughing and sneezing, the light click of the tongue she makes at the end of every sentence, a period so to speak; you work your way through the mountain of reports, of newspapers, in order to feel close to her, the seeming wealth of information creates a feeling of closeness which has to be kept going with even more reports, articles, analyses; accelerating, reading even more, isn't possible since from the very beginning you were in a rage to plow your way through them word by word, a rage, yes, a rage, for your despair is accompanied by a strength, a strange energy which allows you to sit through nights, days without eating, always searching for the piece of information that will bring release

———

Corpses were thrown into wells and rivers. When the bodies surfaced at other places, they were slit open and filled with stones and sand to keep them submerged. A few were carried downriver to a factory that had smelting furnaces. Workers dragged them inside, took the gold and silver fillings out of their teeth and cut off their fingers when they couldn't remove the rings. Three men kept watch outside the factory entrance while two burned the bodies in the furnace; later they made the remains into cattle feed.

Your driving force, hope, makes you regret having to sleep, eat, drink, *to interrupt* the search, as does the mixed feeling in your belly, the *potpourri* of excitement, expectation, fear, curiosity and desire for knowledge, but then the reports start to repeat themselves and your responses become dulled, what you read loses its meaning and with meaning also loses its credibility: why should something have happened to Fahrie of all people, perhaps she was in one of those trucks at first but then managed to escape, after all there are people who managed to survive, *witnesses!* If they could, why not her? And you ignore those who were stuck up to the neck in a pit of cement, those who, while unconscious, had their ears, noses and tongues cut off, those whose families were rounded up and thrown on a pile of wood to be burnt alive; you skip over reports of infants being found in a cement mixer, the oldest just two years old, of a large family buried beside a bridge, only found because hands were sticking out of the ground, some with crosses cut into their chests and foreheads, knives stuck through their chins and tongues and the backs of their head missing; you skip over in order to survive, don't you? — *All nine corpses had their throats cut and all body hair burnt off. One of the victims had been scalped and the eyes taken out. Another victim had no skin on the left elbow. The spine of a third body was broken. That there was a grave at this place was indicated by the fact that it was regularly visited by friends and family. Weeds had been cleared and flowers planted in various places.* Laughable, how laughable, you think, flowers, you laugh to emphasize how laughable it is, weeds seem permissible in the face of death, in the face of mass death flowers are merely absurd, garden gnomes in the void, in the face of the catastrophe your grief is meaningless, your loss no loss, your loss meaningless, no more than a scratch, a bruise, how can you have the audacity to get all worked up, to complain of injustice, to focus on your own needs, what is your grief compared with that of the majority,

32

given the war, Fahrie has lost the right to insist on being found; you're ashamed, and not just once; it's a condition, a degenerate condition that brings you closer to yourself at the same time distancing you from yourself, so that your condition, your shame, seems to keep starting up time and again, *endlessly*, because you've never stopped feeling ashamed.

You see pictures of the mass grave in Ovčara, most of the bodies exhumed but scarcely recognizable as such; at first sight it's just a lot of white garbage bags spattered with soil, piled on top of each other, spilling into each other, tangled up, gigantic entrails; only when you look more closely can you distinguish shoes, legs, hands, heads, you can see that some had tried to protect themselves from the shots, that they all fell and their weight pressed them together into a kind of *single* corpse; they even have to share death, they don't have one of their own, just the communal death: their murder happened so quickly that in death they are no longer individuals, their bodies were *one* battlefield, the killing was carried out anonymously, infecting the killed, making them anonymous too; thus they are *one* death and their surviving family and friends are *the* mourners, a mourning mass, not a mourning individual.

It becomes clear to you that you are part of this mass, the continuation of the *series* of victims, it becomes clear to you as you pick up Fahrie's photo and think back for a moment to the day when you took her picture, on a hill near your house, the sun behind her already setting, the strong breeze making the meadow rustle and the sunlight reflected on the individual stalks, lots of tiny, pointed suns, you remember the quivering grass made you think of waves, a green sea, and nothing could destroy your peace, that's what you thought; a few months later —

War. Victims and soldiers, no one can remain a human being

in war, or can they? If we're borderline creatures, if we have borders all the time and on all sides but no single border in one particular direction, then crossing old borders and setting up new ones is in our *nature*, we even live in a border zone, for God's sake, the future, at the same time the past and present, dammit, you swear, and even death is just a border, a movable border; what you don't say is that you feel it's almost as normal, or should I say *human*, to try to break down the borders of life, of survival, as the borders of killing —
Pornography. Perhaps the murdering as well as the mass raping was filmed, dubbed and sold for entertainment purposes or as souvenirs, as a memento of once having felt alive, everyday life was too monotonous, *drained of reality*, dying a little more each day; it only seems possible to be truly alive in resistance to the world.

It hardly occurred to you that you might have been done an injustice. From your point of view, the abduction of your wife is a mistake which can be easily rectified, just give her back, you say, and all those years of waiting won't have been in vain. Naturally you've quite often asked yourself: why Fahrie, of all people, and at the beginning you were angry, you felt like shouting abuse at anyone and everyone, knocking them flat, anyone and everyone was to blame, but over the years there was one question that refused to go away: *What do we really know about the person we love?*
The situation? — no, the war's not to blame, the war announced its approach long before, its arrival wasn't a surprise, neither for you nor for your family, a storm after the downpour, bad weather, that's all. And death? In wartime dying is avoidable, to be among the dead is a *bit of bad luck*. War, supposedly an *extended duel* with all means available to the extreme of *total defenselessness*, complete will-fulfillment, so keep stepping it up. What was that about mutual suicide? Oh

no, it was *abstract mass murder* people were talking about, slaughtering from a comfortable distance, effortlessly piling up mountains of corpses. And the aim? Eternal *peace* and, of course, revenge for the acts of destruction; the idea of using passive resistance to arouse a sense of shame and thus reduce violence is ridiculous, after all humans are mass creatures with mass souls and mass instincts, with a preprogrammed mass reaction to particular structures, in this case aggression, so step up the hostile feeling, the hostile intent, or both; basically it doesn't matter, the result's the same: fear; initially a vague fear, though bound up with a specific expectation, the expectation of losing more than one thought one possessed, the expectation of dying and seeing people die.

But if war is a duel, you thought, it must be possible to avoid it. It isn't your fight, it wasn't your fight, it would have been possible, would have been desirable to flee, the only sensible thing to do in a war that isn't your war, isn't to your way of thinking, but Fahrie wanted to stay, refused to flee even though you asked her, begged her to repeatedly. Not only would she not listen to you, she went on at you, she couldn't understand why you were so uninvolved, indifferent, it's your country, she said, they haven't got the right to ban our culture and our language, to close down our newspaper, our radio, television and the university in Prishtinë, don't you realize that almost eighty percent of the population have to leave the country to find work? They were fired because they were Albanians. Rugova's right, she said, and followed his call, boycotted elections, refused to pay taxes, went to secret meetings by night to set up hospitals, clinics where they didn't refuse to treat you, by day to secret schools to give lessons in a room with up to sixty pupils, disrupted again and again by police, spies; eventually the time and place of classes was only decided for the next day and spread by word of mouth. She helped to turn schools into refugee camps, student

35

demonstrations on the streets of Pristina, two busloads of police armed with truncheons, teargas and live ammunition, Fahrie had to flee and hide at home; yet she still carried on, made up little packages for New Year and Christmas with presents, chocolate, books, pencils, marbles and teddy bears to distribute to schools and Orthodox churches, the children don't need to be enemies, she said, and continued to fight *for our cause*, against your will, and you started to look the other way, perhaps you also admired her, respected her; anyway, you were out of the country, you *couldn't* have intervened even if you'd wanted to, you had enough to do earning money for her and your family, you had enough to do on the building site by day, at the hotdog stand by night, enough on your plate with the immigration service, residence permit, visa; you were afraid of losing the three-story house in B., your vegetable garden, the roses and wild orchids by the house wall, the car in the garage, the warm summer winds on the balcony and the voices of the stream in late autumn. You were happy, there was no reason to protest, not for you.

It was her fault that she was abducted, that's what you think and what you thought immediately after she was arrested, even if you don't say it out loud, never will say it out loud, it was her own fault, she brought it on herself, on herself and on you, and then the thought gets stuck there, becomes a formula which repeats itself automatically, day after day, soon hour after hour: she didn't care about you. She didn't think of you, only of herself, of her *cause*. What a kind of selfishness, you think, what a kind of selfishness not to consider that you're not only harming yourself but your family as well, that if you're injured, you're not the only one to feel the injuries, you pass them on, much enlarged, and their consequences. How could you blame the war when all it did was to *be there more and more*, how could you blame it when it announced it

was coming, when it invited you loud and clear to get out of its way —
and you start to hate her. You hate her for her stubbornness, her lack of consideration, her selfishness, for putting your happiness at risk and losing it. You hate her for allowing herself to be abducted, for not being stronger, quicker, smarter so she could avoid being arrested; for preferring, perhaps even now, to fight for *her cause*, it's not yours! instead of getting in touch with you to tell you she's all right and you don't need to worry any longer. You hate her because you can't stop loving her, even though you've been trying for ages, because all your attempts to banish her from your life ended in failure since she'd already been banished, though not by you, *that's* what makes the difference, *you* want to be the one who does the banishing, not the one who suffers from the banishing. Suddenly you see *yourself* as the one abducted from Fahrie's life and her as the one who arranged the abduction, the tables turned, in a strange way *meaningfully*, and you hate her for making you disappear, without asking you, and you'd like to see her again, just once, to say farewell and to tell her that you didn't deserve to stay missing for seven years.

Then you stop searching because it seems wrong to you to demand answers; instead you ignore the reports in which survivors recount how all those *who could read and write* were systematically killed, you think up escape stories, fantasies in which Fahrie managed to buy her freedom with a hundred German marks which, going from hand to hand, miraculously managed to find their way to her: a backpack by the edge of the road perhaps, filled with money, several years' savings forgotten or stolen during flight; the procession of those abducted approaches the spot, Fahrie's standing right beside it, the soldier orders her to carry her belongings, not to put anything down, she obeys, naturally; she's afraid and picks up

the backpack, takes the money that she only finds later, when she's in the camp —
on three sides the camp is enclosed by a six-foot barbed-wire fence, on the south side by a wall of corrugated iron; on the west side, beside the main entrance, is a house that is used alternately as an office and a barracks; on the north and east the camp's guarded by two towers, tall as trees, with searchlights and floodlights; the barns, formerly used to store grain, are now detention cells with beds of straw and damp grass; forced labor out in the fields, in the cowsheds, from first light until nightfall; meager rations, a loaf of bread for thirty people, supper a bowl of watery bean soup; Sunday's visiting day: civilians in the camp, they're allowed to kick the prisoners, spit at them, attack them; interrogations every day, the same questions all the time: whether they have any weapons, whether they would vote for independence in a referendum, whether they would go back to their village after the end of the war. To the first question Fahrie answers no, to the other two yes, for which she gets hit in the face, kicked in the stomach.

One night the floodlights fail, a *piece of luck*, Fahrie steals along past charred cowsheds, burnt-out shacks into the darkness, hurries past the detention cells, past the guards' quarters till she reaches the main building. By that time the short circuit has been mended, she just has time to slip through a door — the watchtower searchlights miss her by a fraction of a second — but then two soldiers are blocking her way. Quickly she hides in a dark corner, waits (she seems to feel her heart pounding all over) till it's clear again, then heads for the office of the commandant —
who is *incredibly* venal, of course: a piece of paper in exchange for three months' salary, no, seven, no, four, no, five, the bargaining amuses him, he's almost astonished as he signs her

certificate of release, *what a fearless woman*, and shakes his head, his appetite has been sated for that night so he lets her go without even propositioning her —

free at last: and Fahrie runs, runs, runs, a boat by the bank, no oars, she paddles through the wet with nothing, the boat is like paper, collects water, she only just, only just manages to reach dry land.

Forgotten vegetables, vegetables, the only things that are truly neutral, even animals are slaughtered indiscriminately, cows, goats, sheep, but the potatoes grow as if nothing had happened, nonpartisan leaves, Fahrie gathers them, eats them, even raw they're better than watery soup, screams after sunset, every day there are fewer of them, *and then there were three*, better than all that, there's just a hike through forests and mountains left, Macedonia at last, at last she's free —

free and alive, what else could she be, you think, forgiving her for not having sent you a sign of life so far, how could she anyway, she was probably sent from camp to camp or none of her messages reached the right recipient, chaotic, you say, at the time everything was chaotic, it was normal for letters, telegrams to go astray, even now, you say, it can happen even now; then you fall silent, overcome with the fear that you might be wrong, she could have actually died, not while fleeing but on the very night she was taken away, abducted before the eyes of her family, simply shot, executed, a bullet in the head, then dumped in a pit, like all the rest —

and you are overcome with *unseemly* public grief in the coffee house, in the supermarket on the corner, while working at the hotdog stand, you're weeping — once more or still? — but you are ignored, as if mourning has made you invisible: the newspaper vendor's still walking up and down, the lovers are still whispering sweet nothings in the corner. You stick your handkerchief in you breast pocket, as if you intend to go and

cry somewhere else. When you finally stand up, you walk carefully, as if the tears had left your body more vulnerable, lighter, your steps soundless —
for grief has its own four walls, is that not so?

At our second meeting, old eyes grow over new ones, they grow at the moment when I notice that I can see, can actually see, not images scurrying, hurriedly slipping past, but feeling, gently touching them instead; the delay in processing perception doesn't bother me, it surprises me, but it's a familiar feeling, it's concealed in past images I don't like remembering, the memory itself healed over.
I promise to help you, I, who am helpless myself, who barricade myself behind events, the lives of others, who have no better way of dealing with things than to let chance take its course, I trust it. We're on our way to the subway station, it's three in the morning, we've been walking around and around the park talking about life; no more questions, you said, and I stuck to that; we walked around and around the park talking about the world, uttering commonplaces, and watching the places become towns, the towns cities and the cities countries, we gave the countries names and set up a world in which there is little, but above all ourselves; see how easy it is, we said.
Soon we'll say goodbye, tired, inside our heads only words of one syllable and the question of when I will see you again, we're not there yet, we're still standing by the taxi stand, hesitant, marking time, waiting for a taxi. I'll drop you off at your apartment, I say, thanks, you say, and just before I get into the taxi, a stray kiss brushes my cheek.

3

Five o'clock doesn't come a fraction of an inch sooner, the
hands are resting on the clock face as if dead. Now it seems
clear, in the early morning, when sleep is expected, you can't
do anything but think of *her*, but imagine — bells ringing in
the distance, cars roaring past, steps crunching on gravel
looking up at the clouds, neatly raked all around flowerbeds
— what your first meeting will feel like; but wait for her call, a
monsoon for parched ears, although she doesn't know your
number, mistaken belief, mistaken feeling, uncontrollable.
Your loss takes on a life of its own, grows and grows, a weed,
a boundless, monstrous growth, comfortable, gluttonous and
fat, uncontrollable, see above, sucking the life out of the
ground under all other emotions, for emotions too have their
ground, you say, a life underground, roots and worms; is that
the reason why missing her is both action and feeling because
as an emotion it goes its own way, develops its own
momentum which is beyond influence, beyond control, a
hybrid form, emotion and activity at the same time? —
and sickness, chronic yearning, brought on by an excess of
affection. Naturally the degree to which you miss someone
depends among other things on how much emotion you have
invested in the missing person, on whether you're willing to
go so far as to lose your whole investment, on whether you
can go that far. And *it* is devious in the extreme, initially it
hid, under cover of a codeword, " I miss you" = "I love you
very much," slipped under the dog-ears of autograph albums,
which were only aired if, hopelessly unscrupulous, one
ignored the warning: "Top Secret"; basically a spy who
wanted to check whether it was safe to leave the realm of
dog-ears: to miss someone seems harmless — although it
could be a mutation you're dealing with, *mutated* love.

Missing someone or something is a form of remembering, you say. It's dependent on the quality of one's memory; if one forgets easily, one misses things less. This is an equation that doesn't work out, you can sometimes miss people, situations you've never been acquainted with, you were never allowed to get into; in that case you're missing the idea of something that never existed in reality, you're not missing something that is immensely important, and precisely because it never became real, you can't give up the feeling of missing it.

You once said that missing someone was like a black-and-white photograph which had been unwillingly and crudely colored in so that some colors caught the eye more than others, while some parts were almost invisible, and didn't you say something about a stench, a terrible stench that followed you, not just while you were walking past the manhole cover? None of that comes close to describing it, does it? After all, missing someone is slowly losing them while fully aware that you are losing them, the way the loss of part of your identity expresses itself, and that explains the waiting, the desperate waiting, hoping to be healed, hoping the separation will be reversed.

So you sit at the window, in which time behaves in a different way from what you were used to until now, and eventually you slip into it. Suddenly there is nothing but time, all activity dissolves in time, is diluted by it, no longer exists or vegetates as a shadow of itself. And that's fine by you, for your whole attention is directed toward the moment of reunion, never toward the first three weeks or years, the more future; that doesn't exist, your future ends with the appearance of Fahrie, no, nonsense, of course it exists, it's just that it's not relevant yet, all your plans are waiting with you, with both of you —
all-powerful waiting: in waiting, duration takes over your life. Duration is ceaselessly splitting up without fundamentally

changing; it preserves and accumulates past time in the present, thus also becoming a memory which draws together a plurality of moments in one. Duration can fuse with itself, but it can also uncover others, suck them up and expand. It checks everything, and everything that draws attention away from it is cut; it's gradually cutting your life down to size. This waiting, you say, is unforgivable.

You worry about our meetings, they have to be as harmless as they're intended, I have to promise never to phone you in the evening, calls between eleven and five in the afternoon are unsuspicious, semi-suspicious those during lunchtime, it could be prearranged. Actually I'd prefer you not to phone me at all, you say, I will call, from a public telephone, we must avoid written records of any kind; I would also prefer it, you say, if you didn't write me any letters, send me cards. You make me promise never to wear perfume, my scent might linger on you. Before you leave my apartment, you brush your clothes, no hairs, you say, there mustn't be any hairs for anyone to find; when you wash your hands, you always use the soap you gave me, the same brand as you use at home. I rarely go to your place, mostly you come to mine, and I know that every time you take a different route to the subway, sometimes even avoid the subway, preferring roundabout routes with buses and streetcars. You make sure that we never enter or leave the building together, a certain time must always elapse between us. I know that after our meetings you always go for a half-hour walk to rid yourself completely of my smell. We always meet at different times, your favorite is late morning since the streets are empty at that time, the neighbors out at work, and you fool curious glances through slightly raised curtains by pulling your hood or your cap low down over your face. Finally, as the ultimate safeguard, you ask me to swear that, should Fahrie ever hear about us, I will assure her that we were just good friends, nothing more.

At home it sets in, *an ungrateful feeling* —
I call moments to mind, I'm not being petty, assign significance as it suits me, a glance, the way it's switched off, fades, the *contact* that took place, and I ask myself if I'm justified in assuming more —
then I talk about you to make room for other things, sleep's impossible, eating as well, I have to talk about you, I talk to myself, I have no other ear to hear, spend hours talking, as if it would bring you closer to me; out of fear of losing the *ungrateful feeling*, my microcosm has opened up and expanded, new possibilities, I know they existed before, only I didn't see them before —
some hesitation before the unknown remains, settles in, yet still euphoria.
Rarely am I so close to myself.

Instead, our complicity develops word by word and ends up as a kind of *love at last sight*, for we are accomplices, we no longer communicate by words but restrict ourselves to hints, as if I'd been through the same as you. Of course, I know your story in multiple versions, in all variations, *and it's always the same story*, basically it feels as if it was *I* who had fled not once but thirty times, as if it was *I* who had lost not one but thirty members of my family; astonishment — been there, done that.
It's a comfort to you that I don't deal with you as a victim; in fact, it's more than just a comfort, it's liberating for you that I'm not running a doctor's office where you're a patient and have to recount your medical history, that Fahrie is not taboo for me, that you can talk to me about her *without reservation*, what you have to say is marked out before you say it, the story of the abduction a formula that you repeat, several

44

times a day as if you would find a trail, *the* trail, if you only recited it often enough. The rest of your life has been transformed into plans, which remain empty words, their content doesn't concern you, you just say it to convince yourself that there is life outside this formula.

Sometimes, however, you turn to new sentences to feel more understood: walking between words in outsize letters, we approach the sense step by step, soon dawn is splintering, we hold back our yawns, refuse to go home, and you say, I think Fahrie doesn't actually exist since she's not there in the form of a body. To say she only exists as a thought is an understatement, she's several thoughts, several thoughts at the same time, she's a memory, a mental image, and yet more than just a memory, an image. You have to make an effort to call up the image, it seems to be behind your eyes, in a place you would only see if you could expand and turn your eyeballs. Your memory of Fahrie is concealed in mute images which do not reproduce the remembered event but the feelings you had at the time: memories of Fahrie are memories of feelings for Fahrie. That's why you find it difficult to describe her, the description's there, on the tip of your tongue, but it doesn't satisfy you, so then you try to fill out the lines. But you're aware these are afterthoughts so that they can only be fictional corrections. In truth, to say that Fahrie only exists as a thought is an exaggeration; she only exists in your memories and since you refuse to divulge any of these memories, she doesn't exist anymore.

When she disappeared, you not only lost the person, you also lost the everyday, unspoken repetitions which are part of a home, which are part of you. That leaves the question: how much of her are you, what remains in you after her? And you no longer borrow her words, her thoughts, there's no point to it anymore, you only used to do it to be better understood by

45

her, by *her*.

Her stare sits there in such an unfriendly fashion, my colleagues say, she's so moody! ignoring the appetite I no longer have, leaving me with just stomachache and one ear constantly pricked for the telephone.

While you gradually start pinching my words, swiping my thoughts.

We speak to each other on the telephone every day, you forget your fear that you might be misunderstood, now you feel certain that Fahrie would understand if you explained: the friendship, the search, your pullover, your trousers, a change of underwear in the chest of drawers, your own toothbrush, a few CDs and books, bit by bit your belongings are taking up residence in my apartment, at first it's just the one night you spend on my couch because you've missed the last streetcar and don't want to walk home; at first explanations are important, reasons why saying goodbye, even for just a short while, isn't necessary, can be put off, later you stay at my place as a matter of course, day after day, we're like brother and sister, you say, and you like to be close to me, especially at night.

Unkind sleep: constantly rolling over from one side onto the other, the bed can't be too big, you speak, for lack of secrets you repeat what has been said during the day, more urgently perhaps, and all at once you grasp my hand and squeeze it tight, as if you were afraid I'd disappear, dissolve like one of your dreams. I know I've often told you about this longing I have to turn into air, slowly, very slowly, as if I were being rarified, and one day I wouldn't be there anymore, just like that. Abstruse, you said, that longing's abstruse, what kind of longing is that, making you disappear, shouldn't it arouse the desire never to want to disappear? That's what I call a proper longing. My improper longing confused, then increasingly hurt you, as if not even you could prevent me from being lost, during the day you argued, during the night you went on at me, held my arm and didn't let go, I had to free myself finger by finger, your prints were still visible on my arm the next day.

Would songs have helped you, the songs of your childhood, *Ninulla*, calmed you down? for it only seems possible to sleep if one is calm, not angry like you; all your anger pent up in your sleep, furiously rolling over and hitting out, you hate the world, you'd kick it, stamp on it if you could. No singing would make your anger content to wait for another night, no sung wishes that the child should grow up to be hard working, clever, strong, and brave, more hard working, clever, strong and brave than the nation's greatest hero. They are stories your mother told you, stories of the *Fair One of the Earth*, ruler of the underworld with a three-headed guard dog and black skin that can be peeled off, who sleeps at night cut up into four parts in a treetop; and of the storm-demon Kulshedra, a gigantic being, her face and body covered in gray hair, with a long tail and nine tongues, who inhabits the wellholes in the mountains, makes the water dry up and only releases it when a person has been sacrificed to her, that's why there are skulls outside the cave; sometimes, however, when she's in a good mood, she advises heroes and hands out oracles; or of the Drangues, whose whole life is devoted to combating Kulshedra and who come into the world as animals or human beings. As humans they wear little felt caps and hide two or four wings under their armpits, their hearts are made of gold and they die if their shirts are destroyed. They combat the storm-sprite by hurling trees and rocks at her, but Kulshedra defends herself with deadly urine. And Emine says, *it was the way it was*, and you say, *may everything turn out well*, a ritual as much as her closing words: *Let the story go into the earth, health into us.*

You remember your childhood, the things you mother used to say, the way her voice rolled and gurgled, in those days not yet dull, subdued, not yet hoarse, worn out; you remember its rhythm, the quiet, lolloping drumbeat of her sentences, damdamdam-da, damdamdam-da, you can hear them buzzing in your ear, and at the end of the story, Emine starts to whisper, to speak slowly with lots of pauses, there's a hissing sound as she tells it, a hissing and puffing, a railroad engine

—

and until recently you used to tell me fairy stories if I couldn't get to sleep, an odd habit for grownups, I said, and at first refused to listen, what have they to do with me, these skulls desperate to get married, rolling off in search of a wife at every opportunity since they're actually enchanted princes, or these forgetful woodcutters who lose water-sprites to ponds because they neglected to conceal their tail fins and scaly shirts; what do I care about Lugát, the *restless spirit* who creeps out of his grave at night, breaks anything made of glass — windows, jugs — beats up the neighbors and distributes nightmares; and I was right, it wasn't what you were saying that gripped me but the sound of your voice, the change in it when it felt at home: your Albanian, firm ground, an incantation with just a beginning and an end, nothing in between, sometimes one or other of the words coming to a halt on its own; a secret language which should only be whispered, its sounds only suggested, or is it a language with puppy fat, sounding just a little chubby?

Your Albanian is undulating, hills and valleys alternate. And then it purrs, as an animal it wouldn't be a tiger, rather an anteater. Its color would be yellow ochre, it has the leisurely quality of sand blown by a sluggish wind. It would be a round shape, a sphere with lots of breasts and short legs, a creature that never runs, always crawls, yet hardly ever stumbles. It has short arms that it seldom uses, perhaps to swing them about, but most of the time they dangle down, especially when it's tired and, yes, its fur is the color of sand.

Beside you a cassette recorder, recorded is your own voice, words you stole from your bedtime reading *at the well lapdogs swinging in sadness on the shoetree are chatting full of sugar candy*. You left out some words when you read it, now the book thinks it's getting its own back by whispering absurdities to you, but you're grateful for the distraction, grateful for every line *by mistake Auntie cooks slightly leafless basilisk*.
Silence, the tape's finished, *ants also are low-dream beasts*; you move on to assigning dates to events, producing memories, most important of all: the chronology. You feel the need to give your life a new history; above all events but also objects are labeled with time, day, month, year, then the place and two empty anecdotes; after that the waiting seems suppressed whenever you get up for a few minutes to catch up on dates that were omitted, even if there is nothing.

Where to start the search. You refuse to read reports, whatever they are; you refuse to read. You don't want to hear anymore, not about prisons, not about women's camps, you evade my question *How much do you know?* by pretending to know nothing. It's the survivors I'm interested in, you say, not the dead. So I read secretly, slipping books, reports under bedcovers, cushions, pullovers if I hear a noise, your noise; I snatch at scraps of words, they fight back, unexpectedly, perhaps it's not so much the words that are fierce though but rather the images, images which fix themselves in my mind, and I call them up, it's unavoidable, I feel compelled to, they won't go away from my inner eye, I see interrogations, rapes, executions, go past schools, police stations and hospitals, single and mass graves at building sites with cranes, cement mixers and excavators, and I think, how convenient, everything was there already, it just had to be put to a different use.

The images don't go back onto the pages of hundreds of reports, they stick inside me; it was a mistake to imagine them.

First dead-end: she, the woman you miss so much, is present in every sentence you speak, in every pause you make, consciously or unconsciously, in which you feel you've been caught out because for a brief moment you weren't thinking of her; how can we find a person whose existence is at the very least *doubtful?* We *must* believe she's still alive.

We surf the Internet, typing Fahrie's name into search engines and going through every result one by one, there aren't that many, her name and a few pictures on the webpage of *mailorderbrides.com.* She can be ordered, you say with a beaming smile, that makes the search simpler, but is that really her, I ask, and you immerse yourself in the blurred photo, reduce it, enlarge it, now you're looking at a thigh, now Fahrie's twin is as small and thin as a pencil.

I am a woman with experience, I was married and now I'm a widow, in the summer I like swimming in the river or lying in the sun. I prefer sunny weather because I prefer wearing lightweight clothes. I don't like people jostling, I don't like noise, I prefer to spend my time with my husband. I like children and they like me; when I'm with them, I become a child myself. I like animals, horses and dogs, in the winter I like a fire, wood, soft music, quiet and rain. Do you really expect to find Fahrie or are you just searching so as to escape the waiting? *I have various interests, my hobbies include tennis, photography, ancient history, classical music. I love French and Italian cooking. On the one hand, I am frank, practical and determined, on the other, I'm a hopeless romantic.* She'd never say things like that, you say, my wife is a very down-to-earth person, French food, you say and laugh. *I like dancing, I like nature, baking and cooking. I'm home-loving, affectionate, quiet, intelligent, warm-hearted, romantic and hard working. I'm looking for an affectionate, tender, reliable, decent partner who would like to have children.* They all sound the same, you say, how can I distinguish one from another? *My hobbies are music, dancing, the sea, travel and reading. I'm honest, romantic, and tender. I would like an intelligent, well-educated, sensible, self-assured husband with a good sense of humor for a happy life together. I am an affectionate, optimistic woman with a sense of humor, who would like to fall in love and start a family.*

Perhaps she's there, perhaps she's not, you say, the things they say don't help me. Have a good look at the pictures, I say, surely you'll recognize her? That hairstyle's wrong, you say, those clothes are wrong, but those are things a person can change, I say, what about their faces, their bodies? Unclear, blurred, you mutter.

What you don't say is that with the years Fahrie's face has moved out of your memory and down to a deeper level, which changes with your mood; sometimes you think you can remember every detail, at others it's so hazy that you feel you're losing her image, or herself, for what is she apart from an image? —

and, you object, wouldn't she come back to me before inserting such an ad?

Second dead-end: a visit to the psychiatrist, a white room, flowers in vases, flowers in pots (pot-life with support prostheses) and hangings on the wall with neatly trimmed patches of color, innocuous.

It's quite possible, he says, that Fahrie is refusing to return to her old life, that she's ashamed of having been tortured. It could be, he says, that she's assumed a new identity since her old identity was destroyed in that extreme situation.

Mind and body, the doctor says, reflect the kinds of torture that were used. Frequent effects are gastrointestinal disorders, injuries to the rectum, the skin, pain in the joints, atrophy of the brain, heart-lung disorders, damage to the middle ear, and a reduced pain threshold. Frequent psychological effects are depression, fits of aggression, sleeplessness, nightmares, psychotic episodes, confusion, feelings of guilt, instability, irritability, introversion, poor concentration, loss of the sense of direction, memory lapses, headaches, hallucinations, disturbed vision, alcohol incompatibility, dizzy spells, and sexual disorders. In the long term, people who have been tortured are troubled by severe states of panic, which often arise suddenly; they feel different from the rest, different from their surroundings, from people who have not undergone that experience, they feel guilty for surviving, overcome, and reduced in their *being*.

What you must understand, he says, is that most victims cannot get back to their previous identity, which they urgently need if they are to continue living. They are damaged people, some describe themselves as undead, *night after night I die but I always end up alive again*, incapable of developing relationships. Their perception of reality is disturbed, others always represent a threat to them, so they live in isolation, incapable of talking about what they have experienced. They remain stuck in the role of victim, in a cruel memory which is beyond their understanding of the world, humanity and normality, their old life no longer exists, nothing is the way it was, everything is questionable, things that are a matter of course become suppositions, suppositions highly doubtful. Their pain, basically a specific moment, therefore a *historical event*, repeats itself day after day, thus becoming an endless experience.

Linguistically reduced to sounds of no great meaningfulness

while being tortured, the victims have to learn to speak again, to reacquaint themselves with their bodies and those of others whose movements indicate a different, normal context. They have to entrust themselves to the world once more. If your wife has been through the things you describe, she would be more susceptible to illness, the doctor says, she would suffer from moods of depression, emotional imbalance, a lack of drive, headaches, a bad back, stomach pains, disturbed sleep, and psychosomatic disorders such as skin diseases, stomach ulcers, or even cancer could appear.

But, he assures us, it's impossible to generalize, the effects of torture differ from one person to another, I don't know Fahrie's personality, she could be the last person to deny her previous life and look for a new one. The answer to your question lies in her character —

we seem to have run out of possibilities, your mother's the only one who believes the truth can be read in coffee grounds, every week she travels to a fortune teller in the southwest of Kosovo, three hours there, three hours back.

You hesitate for a long time before you ask me: Would you call Kosova for me? It's a delicate question, you want to avoid my suspicion that you only made friends with me in order to get me to make this call. Who? I ask. Your former colleagues, you say, you worked in the office for missing persons there. You want me to call Sam? I ask. Who? you ask. He's the one who identifies the bodies they find, I say.

You don't reply. You're hurt because I don't believe Fahrie will be found alive.

Next morning the line to Pristina is engaged at first, half an hour later it's free.

4

We meet at the airport. Limp, sad the hand you flap; not taking care of myself, you say, even now I'm still not used to cooking; you wanted to leave, reflected on weaknesses, *and I on landscape.*

A building site outside the window, an extra row of seats stuck to the wall, the buzz of passengers at our feet, and we don't telephone, we don't read or sleep, don't eat, don't listen to music or go for a walk, not even around and around in circles; we're waiting for the feed-point or the *Paradise* to open. Time is our enemy now that we're waiting, sitting and waiting, a table between us with an empty plastic bottle, the silence doesn't force itself on us, it reigns and I read signs, again and again, until you break the silence, which is no silence, and say thank you for coming; of course, I say, how could I have refused? your call early in the morning, your voice, slight, falls close to my ear, as if you were standing beside me and in a whisper you say, they've finally found her

—

they've found Fahrie.

How are you?

Not good, you say.

Now at last you know for certain, I say, you wanted to know for certain.

My encouragement drops into a void; I would have caught it, had I meant what I said.

You remain silent.

I'm very sorry, I say; you interrupt, would you go with me? you ask, would you accompany me to Prishtinë? I don't feel like going there by myself.

No, I say, I'd rather not —

at this — perhaps that's what I was waiting for — your pleading assails me, please, please come with me.
When do you have to be there?
I'm flying next week, you say, you're expecting a beating from the family, they've been brooding over it for seven years since Fahrie disappeared; you went away, too noticeably, not in accord with propriety, what will the neighbors say, your mother's first question, the mourning period not yet over and you? What mourning, you asked, what mourning? she's not dead, you said, why then mourn for her? off she went, out of the door, then silence until that telephone call, yesterday, seven in the morning, perhaps half-past six, you don't look at the clock, there's crackling on the line, a whooshing noise in your ear, then, quiet but crystal clear, they've found Fahrie, come home, we want to bury her; your nose itches, aches, and your legs tumble down, several hundred miles it seems to you.

Where was she found? I ask, and when? Near Prishtinë, you say. And the cause of death, is the cause of death known?
You remain silent.
You say you didn't ask.
The funeral, I ask, when is the funeral planned for?
A whooshing in the receiver, a rhythm that continues, two words, whoosh, two words, whoosh, two words, whoosh, no more is necessary; very soon, you say, Mother's organizing it, you say, please come.

Wardrobe and dress untouched, suitcase closed, I call back, do you really want me to come with you, are you sure? Your voice sleepy, throaty, grabs me by the back of my head, of course I want you to come, we're going in a week's time. I want to say, that's not a good idea, go by yourself, please, go by yourself, but then I discover that it's a farewell, there's nothing to keep you here anymore —

so I say, a deposit, hoarse in my throat, I'll come; you say thanks and hang up.

The idea that she could be dead, could really be dead, that you're not just saying it, that you feel it as well, becomes clearer with every second, driving a wedge into the rest of the present.

You use your hands when you speak, often tripping over words, getting in a muddle, your tongue stumbling as if on cobbles, only partly managing to clamber from one stone to the next; you take a deep breath, a disguised sigh, fix your gaze on the carpet, hollow-eyed, the brightness missing. A faint rustling brings you back into the present, you sigh, breathe out, shipwrecked, desperately trying to keep your head above water, all you're interested in now are the details.

Aunt Vlora has been asked to find a bride for you, she has a particular reputation as a matchmaker, she doesn't make mistakes, she can look back on a procession of happy couples. She's come over today, is sipping coffee on the balcony, holding her cup in one hand, the other armed with a pencil writing down the names of possible candidates; whether they are willing is another matter altogether. Emine, Lukja, and Nusha are only too keen to hear her advice, the men have congregated around the TV but you have to stick it out, Vlora wants a description of your dream wife, she keeps probing and probing, doesn't give up, what does she look like? the color of her hair, of her eyes, how tall, slim, fat? you just mutter, pretty, then you agree to dark hair, which is particularly welcome to your mother who has brown curly hair herself, and finally, finally, there's a short list of three girls and you're dismissed; you didn't say much, just "brown hair" and "husky voice."

Vlora worms her way into the families of her chosen candidates on false pretenses: she's looking for work, she's a good seamstress, do they need tablecloths, embroidery, crocheting? at the same time asking, as casually as possible of course, about the daughters of the family, happily counting faces and making mental notes. Finally there's only one left, Fahrie, dark curls dangling down over her forehead, and her voice seems to sound husky, husky enough; now it's Uncle Berat's turn.

Berat, never at a loss for words, praises his nephew's qualities to the skies. At each of the three visits — three are necessary to convince Fahrie's family of your suitability — he keeps drumming it in that you are brave, intelligent, hard working, able to provide for a family, each time worried that her family's answer might be: *Fahrie's too young to marry.* No, they say, you're to give her time, a good answer, as Berat knows, and already he's looking at possible dates for a meeting to announce the engagement.

Now you start to get interested in her after all, this girl, Fahrie, and although you make a pretense of only listening with half an ear, you scribble her name on the palm of your hand and on a letter you get secretly delivered to her: Would she like to meet you, before the engagement if possible? She answers yes, absolutely.

Your nerves exposed, quickly you look around for something, anything to cover them up, past the *quebaptore*, the cook in the window looks as if he's holding up the roof, *a Mini-Atlas in Pristina*, the city a dungeon in the pale light of the evening sun and you are a little worried you might have missed her, or did you agree on something different, not a thread in the buttonhole? Ninety-seven, you're sure it was in ninety-seven, Fahrie twenty at the time, you twenty-one, or was it a year earlier, ninety-six, Fahrie nineteen, you twenty? A stray dog is sniffing the street corner, spiders are weaving autographs around the flower pot, you let your fingers stroll across the table, feeling your way from the middle to your cigarettes when Fahrie arrives, fine drops in her hair, on her coat.

No chilblains by midnight, timidly holding hands, anchors being weighed again, a smile rubbed into your faces. An arranged meeting four weeks before the arranged marriage, but still molehills at every step.

Your first kiss behind the apple tree your secret, a compromise, outwardly the wedding is to remain a compromise, it seems more sensible to both of you to leave all the details of loving, of falling in love, until the catch has been made clear, its size no longer subject to change; everything, you repeat, everything could make it shrink after the first confession and at once the happiness you've just found would start to shrivel. You're both aware of this danger, you've both been in love before, you keep your distance, each following the other around the family pond without being caught —

and something does seem to be growing, it wants contact, a warm nest, just a few days to go, you tell each other, until then: just tugging at nearness.

What a secret: the loving couple, that is the point of the engagement, are indeed in love. But they act as if they're unimpressed, reluctant, with their families busily buzzing around them, two clouds of mosquitoes, on one side, the mothers and fathers, aunts and uncles; on the other, sisters, brothers, and cousins, the getting-to-know-each-other ceremony drags on, wax runs down the candles, forming rivulets, the ventilator does its bit and the shoeshine boys on *Rruga Nënë Therese* wait in vain for customers that night.

In the living room meanwhile, nudges, a rubbing of thighs, expressions of friendship from future relatives. You slip away, just a moment for a squeeze of the hands should be possible,

and disappear into the garden, lean against each other in the blind spot by the toolshed, formerly the outhouse, a cracking noise two yards further on, you separate quickly, Fahrie runs off; only a tramp, she thinks in relief, her look still dazed.
We got married a week later, you say, no one knew we were in love when we got engaged, even today no one suspects anything.

Looking back, you can't really say why you fell in love with her; looking back, her hair seems too dark, her nose too short, her chin too pointed to be attractive, and yet you remember how happy you were, how *incredibly* happy; that can only have been love, you say in astonishment and wonder what exactly did happen. Your memory of the process of falling in love has been erased, all that is left is the result, the state; you remember what happened before and what happened after, but not the time in between, those minutes are missing. I try to reconstruct it, you say, with looks, words, feelings, but in reality I don't know what happened, and that, you think, is why it's so uncanny.
Even now, seven years later, a piece of this past happiness remains inside you, *thin-skinned*. Understandable, for many months there was nothing in your life but that love, it *was* you, you didn't exist anymore. What a gift, what a terrible gift to be able to discard your shell like that, to be able to forget. You felt immortal, not immortal as a person but as if you, still a mortal, had found a moment of immortality.
Is it part of the nature of love to be able to give the illusion of immortality, or is it the memories of love that make it unending?

They keep their heads down as they walk, the lovers, tottering from one tree to the next by the light of the street lamps; officially they're out for a walk, Luan in his village, Fahrie

59

around her house. I don't let up: why the secrecy? I ask. You can't answer my question, you don't know why, you say, our feelings were too precious to share. A wedding, what had a wedding to do with love? marrying was a *transaction*, the acquisition of adulthood by taking over a woman from outside the family, for your Albanian forefathers it would have been quite normal to buy a bride and give the bridegroom a bullet wrapped in straw as a wedding present, a sign that he could kill his wife should she be disobedient. To be married was a piece of good fortune, not least because it was the only way of escaping from the hierarchy of the clan; it was worth trying to find a ritual of your own, something of your own in that crazy clan system. Perhaps, however, it was because you didn't want to talk about something that was still too new, too fresh —

every time it was spoken it might fade, melt, finally disappear, who knows how well it could stand up to curiosity, teasing, pats on the back, who knows whether it wasn't simply an illusion, a mistake that couldn't be corrected if it had been *publicly* discussed in the *family circle*. Naturally people like to declare their love, you say, naturally they do, but as long as they're not sure, it remains whispers exchanged in private and every whispered word merely seems to augment the feeling of being in love.

Fahrie cheats, gets others to sew, embroider, crochet her trousseau for her (tablecloths, undershirts, socks, shirts, towels for her new home and her new family), but despite this, she has an awful lot to do during their short engagement: order the wedding dress, the veil, the blouse, and jewelry to go with it, bridal stockings and shoes, a complete bedroom suite (bedstead, mattresses, sheets and quilts, pillows, woolen blankets) — and cry, three days before the wedding, tradition requires it.

Again the bride cheats, gets around tradition and custom with crocodile tears before the big day, has a smile under her skin; finally, hours before the event, she's dragged into the bathroom, her mother and sisters help to bathe her, her hair is done, her long locks tamed, they have to hang down neatly, a little white hat is set on top, but before that her face is covered in makeup, first of all the foundation, then powder, eye shadow, mascara, bright red lips, her eyes underlined in black, to Fahrie being made beautiful seems to go on forever and it's not finished yet, for now her fingernails and toenails are painted with henna, and not only Fahrie's, but her sisters', cousins', aunts' and mother's as well, they run out of henna, grandmother's thumb is left half pink, if only Emine had bought more of the stuff the day before.

Meanwhile, there are comings and goings in the bridegroom's house: the first guests are greeted with drums and clarinets: your retinue, who are to collect the bride, get into their cars decorated with white hand towels stuck prominently under the windshield wipers; you keep them waiting, your jacket needs mending, you shout from the top floor, they're to set off without you, of course, they shout back, anyway they're desperate to start singing and sounding their horns.

There's singing outside Fahrie's house as well, only women's voices there, accompanied by a tambourine, *our bride is so pretty, oh how pretty is our bride*, they warble, Fahrie herself doesn't know what to think, surrounded by thirty other brides in bridal gowns, with golden bridal bodices, bridal hairdos, and bridal gloves, rival brides, it seems to her and it's only with difficulty that she recognizes her cousins, aunts, and sisters-in-law; some, she thinks, got married four years ago, but no matter, they still curtsey along with her in virginal white.

The convoy approaches, the hooting and bawling can be

heard from afar, *drinks for everyone!* the women welcome the new arrivals with song, meanwhile the bride greets the guests in the traditional way, clasping their hands, making a circle in the air with them, raising and lowering them as if she were praying, and with eyes closed she gives presents to the women of your family: knitwear, jackets, socks, crocheted tablecloths, pot holders, fastens them to their festive clothes with safety pins, to sleeves, breast or side pockets — all that in a shower of rose petals, at least one spot in the world seems to be pink that day. Fahrie is given presents as well, people put gold rings on her fingers, at the end she has eighteen, oh, how few, says Emine, she had thirty-two, but still, with a kiss on the right cheek, a kiss on the left, her beringed hand is held up in the air, the gift can be admired.

You still don't appear, by now no one believes your excuse of a ruined jacket, they're talking of cold feet but no matter, the party continues on its merry way, Fahrie is put in a car, the others are loaded up with everything she's bought in the last months, household goods, bedstead, preceded naturally by a tearful farewell, as if they'd never see each other again, as if the world, the one that was pink just now, were about to end, and this time the bride cries, not crocodile tears, no, she's too brave for that, but she does run to a few communal tears, a decorative embellishment to her cheeks, which get stuck in the powder and hang there, with a friendly glitter; they're hardly visible, her veil is opaque, it protects Fahrie from the evil eye, which is magically attracted by joy, celebrations, and can bring all kinds of misfortune to a family. Father's already throwing candy, children are crawling around in the drive, squabbling in the dust as they search for sweets.

The good wishes to the bride's mother, all the best for your daughter, do not necessarily come from the heart, often envy's at work, there are a few tricks to avoid the evil eye (the standard manual on behavior says: avoid eye contact at all cost or, if someone has stared too long, rub your eyes, that confuses it, distracts it; above all, beware of blue eyes, the lighter they are, the greater the probability that their look is malicious.)

While this is going on, you are at home, uneasy, why the excuse with your jacket? You shake your head, you don't know, nervousness perhaps? Yes, perhaps, you remember your insides were making the celebrations hell for you and they had no intention of calming down, especially not when Fahrie drives up and gets out of the car, only to get back in again after a while to drive on to the restaurant, the women in long evening dresses, the men in dark suits, in broad daylight, the old men with *plisi* on their heads, thin, white caps like half eggshells. There's dancing in the ballroom, the first link in the dance chain your sister, Lumnije, she's holding a red handkerchief and waving it in time to the music. The dance is never-ending and while it's going on the pair of you go to the platform, now another song starts, some clap, others congratulate you, kisses to the right and left, you're sitting at the head of the table under a gigantic heart trimmed with ruches, the ruches pink, the heart red. The celebrations last three days, two days earlier the men were already singing, bawling, roaring, praising your choice of bride: the right choice decides your destiny, *the wrong decision brings disaster.*

Later Fahrie goes around the guests with her nephew on her arm before she jumps over an axe in the meadow and crosses the threshold into her new home, touching it briefly, why? I ask. That's the way she puts her family, her forefathers behind her and establishes contact with our ancestors, you say.

You withdraw to the wedding chamber, it smells of fresh linen, a bunch of wild orchids in the copper bowl beside the bed, they have a heavy scent, your airplanes are dangling from the thread, they've finally flown out of your trouser pockets;

you tread on Fahrie's left foot, squeeze her little finger and ask, following the custom: Who do you belong to, your mother or your father? Neither, she says, I'm wholly yours.

The year before the disaster. Your apartment a room on a fly hunt, the walls bare, the tiles in little heaps on the floor, carefully stacked; as the days pass, photos grow out of the walls, curtains, shelves with books, cassettes, a radio and china figurines, and every Sunday breakfast consists of two fried eggs, two hot chilies, two slices of goat cheese, two slices of tomato on round pieces of white bread with sesame seeds on the crust; after that a walk around the village, the dependable poster on the lamppost, watering the vegetables at three in the afternoon (the pigs are quiet, so no rain again, it's only when they're playing, people say, that they bring clouds, a bit of wind and rain) and in the middle of your conversation a nudge and a wink, no, I certainly don't love you more than my mother, Fahrie says, I know my duty as a daughter.

Not a double life — conforming to custom within the family, the village community, ignoring custom in the anonymity of the city — but an openly Western one: you frequently give rise to talk, the talk an intrusion which makes privacy in public impossible; as you now realize, the conventions enforced by words, glances, and gestures created a sanctuary — without it, it's up to you not to put the desires of society above your own, not to conform with them in overhasty obedience, drumming into you the idea that they aren't the wishes of the group at all, but your own. You must put up with people talking about you, with the fact that the whispers, the hand over the mouth, the surreptitious glances, ostracize you because you are too conspicuous not to cause a scandal.

For many the behavior of both of you is puzzling, worrying: Fahrie's commitment, her training to be a teacher, your unqualified support for her; not even modesty is on your side, modesty's too civilized not to be ashamed of your shame-lessness.

We're landing in an hour, below us cloudy heads, white-haired, tousled, a sea of cloud, beside me your frayed stare at everything that isn't moving, my whispering already too shrill for your senses. Since you've known for certain, you've forgotten how to hear and to speak, you're too profoundly occupied with wishing; wishing that Fahrie hasn't been found, that it's an error, they've got the wrong person, the wrong telephone number, the wrong name, the wrong anything as long as it's a mistake.
You want that so much that you've been writing it, your wish, on little scraps of paper and spreading it all over the apartment, sticking it to the walls, mirrors, telephone, cupboard doors, little incantations, only on paper, true, but they help because they don't cancel out what you've become accustomed to —
suddenly it's enough for you not to know where Fahrie is.
Then you give up trying to wish away the inevitable and you persuade yourself that *it's best the way things are* until you realize that you don't know how stopping works: how to bring missing Fahrie to an end.

Yet it was only last week that the search turned into routine and your conscience was soothed to a certain extent. You write, *at least I know where you are*, a declaration of love of sorts, I find the letter among advertising brochures and bills while you hurry out of the room, allegedly to get some fresh bread. Are you afraid I won't like what I'm reading?
A week has gone by since then and today I hardly dare talk to you, I put it off. Eventually the question refuses to bide its time and bursts out: What am I in the eyes of your family, a traveling companion? You start, my presence is a concern to

you, it has to appear harmless, more you can't say at the moment. Then I have to promise to introduce myself as an acquaintance, working for the Tracing Service.

5

INTERNATIONAL AIRPORT PRISTINA in blue capitals, cracked, the "R" in danger of losing both legs. A small airport, cramped, passport control right next to the baggage conveyor belts, we pick up our suitcases at the same time as our passports are being checked and go out through the exit right beside it, the arrival hall more of an arrival room. Emine has been waiting outside for an hour, she couldn't stand it under the roof any longer, *Mirëdita*, she says, hello, sweltering in the heat. A slalom though the groups hanging around in the parking lot, it's oddly clean, swept, overlarge compared with the airport hut, a faceless bunker even if many-eyed with its blind windows; the grass framed in concrete, its next-door neighbor the United Nations customs office with its blue and white fence, white off-road vehicles with "UN" on them in black, and a throng of horse chestnut trees giving sparse shade; we set off along the mildly warm route.

The windows reflecting the afternoon sky, sun-legs at the edges, your mother, beyond hope, offers withered comfort; at last we know, she murmurs.

During the drive I see meadows, some cultivated, some lying fallow, fields once, now dumps for rust heaps, mangled, dented, abandoned. We rattle past the car sales lot, buzzing like a wasp nest every Saturday, Emine says; the countryside slightly rolling, everywhere new houses, still unoccupied; the bus stops: upside-down yellow feeding bowls.

We talk about unemployment, the low income of your brother Fehmi, a biologist, three hundred euros a month, Emine says, how can one live on virtually nothing at all? Perhaps you don't reply because you have a conscience, you, the eldest son, ought to feed your family, that's the unwritten Albanian law.

On the rat run avoiding the afternoon traffic jam, Italian KFOR soldiers, the tricolor on their armbands, are checking out street sections, grid squares; shortly afterwards two solitary buildings, mere skeletons, cables sticking out of beams, walls, windows, doors, and ceilings missing, the bricks stolen by the neighbors, Emine says, stolen for their own four walls and, indeed, the bricks of the gable are untouched.

A land with little shade, dwarf trees keeping dwarf roots cool, the yarrow on the right has to withstand the sun. Two UN off-road vehicles, a jeep with no license plate, and an excavator on the back of a truck are parked by the ruins, three men in uniform, I think I recognize them as police, two men and a woman with a floppy hat pulled down over her face with sunglasses are walking up and down, eyes on the ground, talking and pointing, they're looking for corpses, Emine says, Serbs used to live there.

At our second meeting, you're still a stranger, you tell me about your family, tell me with your eyes closed —
on the day of her wedding they gave your mother her nephew to hold and made her walk around the family hearth three times: a ritual, first of all she was to provide a son for the clan. The clan, something more than just the sum of all its members, you say, our sense of belonging is strong, every one of us bears the wishes of the clan inside them. On the wedding night, they sing songs about fruitfulness outside wooden doors, while inside the chamber, the wedding chamber, they are working on fruits, hard work, for Emine does not get pregnant, not in the conventional way. In desperation, time is pressing, she goes to see an ancient village crone; if she doesn't produce a child soon, a son please, a son please, she's afraid her husband will replace her.

She's the newcomer in the family, in the next three years she has to prove she's a good mother and *amvise*, housewife. With gaping teeth, billowing trousers, her hair tied back tightly, a green cloth held by a piece of washing line fluttering at her waist, the old woman's hands are aimed at Emine's belly. She recites magic incantations and rubs in a tincture, blue, on a blue day —
the church bells chop up your murmurings, I teeter on my chair, capsize, making the first *contact* possible: happened ages ago, as if just one word were needed —
feelings move on such light feet.

We turn into a side street, hardly wider than the car, we've reached your village. The smell of cow dung and hay comes in through the left-hand window, which is wound down, the right-hand one doesn't work, a bend to the left and we get out, before us a three-story house, a garden full of vegetables, potatoes, tomatoes, chili peppers, and lettuce, among them roses, a patch of grass, bicycles, a ball, a doll. Washing is hanging from a line in the gap in the wall which they intend to replace later on with a picture window, below it the family shoes are resting, a single file that's come to a halt, the shade balancing on narrow steps.
The plaster's missing from your family's house, as it is from most of the houses in Kosovo, your mother's repaired it inside, the interior is in better shape than the exterior. Emine embraces me for a second time, my house is your house, she says, allocating me the role of a distant cousin; that involves rules I don't yet know.
As you explain to me later, rules are omnipresent in Kosovo: how problems within the family are to be resolved, how and when to approach an enemy, the right way to run a household, how dogs are to be treated, what duties each member of the family has to assume, in what order people

can eat; men and women, I come to realize, hardly ever eat together, women eat in the kitchen, men on the balcony or at some other place I haven't yet discovered, however hard I listen; what is special is that customs and conventions have the status of law, you say, they are *ligj* and therefore beyond question.

Emine takes me into the living room, adjusts the flowers in the vase, crutches for elegance, on the wall at the end of the living room a picture of Luan's late father, a bench along the wall, the seat covered with sheepskin; through the window: baby skyscrapers, one next to the other, one like the other, the red bricks bare and none of the interiors fully furnished, uninhabited stone boxes.

When we came back after the war, your mother says, everything had been bombed, it took me seven years to get the house in something like a reasonable state. Plants in every corner, the living room an arbor, a lost soul in it: the TV. Photos of the family, you're there too, Luan as a child, Emine says, with his sister Luminje and his brother Fehmi. Your cue, you appear, at last, yawn, as if you'd been asleep but I heard you walking about, and a baby soon, your mother says, Luminje's going to have a baby. You don't translate everything, you translate lethargically, I give brief answers to save you the bother, Emine gives a helpless smile and suddenly she feels the urge, she's looking for a private conversation; she's speaking Albanian, I know it's about Fahrie, I can hear the name. The change to German is all the more surprising, syllables in quotation marks appear and, out of the blue, the statement *love is weakness*, Emine, eloquent.

A miracle, a submerged island, is approaching: a child is expected, a son, the family hopes. Forty days before it's due, Emine is packed off to her mother-in-law with bag and baggage, she doesn't need to lift a finger, her sister-in-law Nusha, the youngest of the family, gets everything together, piles it up on a sheet, ties it, lifts it onto her narrow shoulders, the things inside shift, pressing into her collarbone and neck, and carries everything down one floor. The received wisdom is that during that period the unborn child is particularly at risk, an unspoken threat, invisible danger, the evil eye again which causes this unease. The only protection is the mother-in-law's equally dangerous eye and her secret room, a paradise of solitude.

Isolated from the world, Emine lives for her womb alone, cares for it, it's more than a womb, a friend, and more than that: a companion, a confidant, an object of love, and provision for her old age. It's an easy life in seclusion, Emine thinks, it wouldn't bother me if the world didn't exist, hers is a small world anyway, the first boundary's the house, the second the garden, the third the village, and what can there be outside the village?

The mother-to-be, still snuggled up in her nest, writes a letter to Nusha: *Get the following things ready in my room: a red silk thread from my right stocking, the midwife's to use it to tie off the umbilical cord after the birth, a sheepskin from the shepherd who brings our milk, a piece of rope from Mother, please ask her for another broom and don't forget to have water blessed by the hoxha. Keep quiet about all this, the fewer who know about it, the less painful the birth will be.* Good little Nusha soon hurries off to carry out the wishes of her sister-by-marriage; she darts across to the shepherd's, orders a fresh fleece, grabbing a bottle of milk as she goes, draws a red thread out of Emine's favorite stocking, wraps it around a piece of paper and puts it in an envelope, trots off to her mother, asks for a piece of rope and a broom, cleans both of them thoroughly, and lays them at Emine's feet while she's sleeping, mouth open, the buzz of a tiny snore coming from her nose.

71

Nusha sighs in protest, gives a little wail, no vise, the sound climbs out of her mouth of its own free will, she has to wait, to wait until her beloved, Fadil, an actor, can marry her, they still need their parents' consent, without it there won't be any wedding. Traditional, Nusha, would like a traditional wedding, the celebrations lasting three days, she wants to be taken to her bridegroom in a procession half a mile long, she'll also hold a little boy in her lap, she hopes she'll have a son too. Fadil, love at first sight, the love of her life — even if it doesn't last all life long, it'll be lovely, a bit of life with Fadil, Nusha sighs, this time on tiptoe and dashes out of the room as a future bride, her thoughts on that oft-recalled first meeting: Nusha in the audience, him on the stage, she keeps herself hidden in the dark, after all, she's only accompanying one of her countless sisters, which one? what does she care, she's out hunting, captures Fadil before his bow; she claps especially loudly, which results in the invitation to the opening-night party, delighted, she bites her lips to make them red and one flirt later he's lost, and so is she because he can't keep his jealousy under control.

Today Nusha's stuffing herself with nuts in frustration, always being told to wait, the fate of the youngest, she's eating them straight out of the tin, what if the same should happen to her as happened to Lula?

Lula, the village maiden: apparently her father, by astute bargaining, had acquired a bridegroom for her, not handsome but sheep-rich, but she had refused even to consider him, no, she did consider and immediately rejected him, she had already found a sweetheart, even though he was already taken. Despite everything, she slept with him, she loved him so why shouldn't she? Lula didn't think much of rules, *love's the only thing that counts, what else?* her lover thought that too and loved her, once, one night, and disappeared; his child remained. A scandal had to be avoided at all cost, the family insisted on an abortion, in secret, Lula was not to bring shame on them, so she was taken to the *shtriga*, the village witch, whose soul, so it was said, shimmered out of her sleeping body at night; then she drank children's blood and ate children's hearts.

One day, when all was quiet, Lula, her mother and grandmother crept to the edge of the village heading for a shack with a black roof, yellow walls and dog roses in the garden, the sickly sweet scent followed them into the house. The *shtriga* had everything ready on the table: an earthenware amphora, a few towels, and hot water. Lula had to lie down on the table, open her legs and bend her knees, the old woman placed the amphora on Lula's lower abdomen, right over the womb. Suddenly Lula's belly started to contract, the pains grew worse and worse, almost unbearable, she felt a stinging, burning, piercing sensation and suddenly the witch felt between Lula's legs and jerked the fetus out.

Some weeks later Lula bought a pair of trousers, a wrist watch, a revolver and a cap, cut off her hair, keeping a few locks, she might need them as a mustache, and swore an oath on the *Kanun* before twelve village elders to live as a man from then on: smoking cigarettes till she was sick of them and drinking the afternoons away in the cafe; staring down women's blouses, however, she left to her buddies.

Blue venetian blinds casting blue light, the vacuum cleaner slumbering in its cardboard box, soft toys sharing the desk, Fehmi's old cup for tennis their meeting point. The walls only recently papered, I scratch at the dried paste, you take my hand, hold it tight. A floral cover on the bed, the worn material tempts the lining to escape even though it doesn't really want to, would prefer to remain inside, too weary to flee. In the bathroom grinning frogs with bowler hats and daisies in their buttonholes, frozen on the toilet paper. No water between three in the afternoon and dusk, too much is used to water the garden.

Your mother, your brother, your nephews and nieces live on the second floor, below them your uncles, aunts, and cousins, not a *kulla*, a fortress from the old days, windowless protection from attack, but a house with normal-sized windows. More than enough: one balcony leads to the next, one sunshade to the next, the balustrade's missing, perhaps next year, if they've saved enough, instead flower pots simulate a barrier to free fall, flowerpots and shoes neatly laid out in a row. A ladder, jammed between the first and second floor is there to prevent a fall, nothing's ever happened, you say to reassure me, only I don't believe you.

Light bulbs dangling from the electric cord, towels, sheets grasped by the shoulders and pegged to the washing line, little footstools on the balcony, floor cushions and short-legged tables for *çaj*, I'm offered a cup, I refuse for fear of saying the wrong thing, of blowing my cover as a harmless acquaintance.

I should really have accepted the invitation, how discourteous to decline a chance to hear the village gossip, actually not so much gossip as disguised chat, abbreviated, condensed speech, in which what has been observed is always there in the conversation: the happenings vouched for are the main content which is commented on either with one longish sentence, or with a look. More isn't necessary, the village is small, the villagers know each other, asking too many questions is indiscreet, a scandal might be uncovered.

Across the street a shrinking farm: the cow is given preferential treatment and drinks out of two bathtubs, one under each birch tree, behind it the turquoise VW with green doors, the farmer, Ali's successor, in his white cap, the *plisi*, at

74

a safe distance. Hens are crawling over the dung heap together with puppies snuffling for things to eat, too little food, most of the dogs will die, Emine says, emptying the remains of dinner, boiled beans and potatoes, into a plastic bowl, which she puts in her crocheted floral bag with the tomatoes, onions, and chili peppers she'll swap for milk and eggs later on.

Emine, always busy, grows five kinds of vegetables in the garden, sweeps and scrubs the house twice a day, also dusts at night, sews and crochets, not for relaxation, no, a traditional supplementary income, *the women's way of earning money*, and at least once a month, for all weddings, funerals, christenings, circumcisions, she would have gone to her parents' home, *the women's way of traveling*, if your grandfather hadn't divorced your grandmother —

the truth is, your mother has survived, larded with *wretchedness*.

Your father Ilir, young, dreamy, dozy, wouldn't have dreamed of spending money, after all, he's poorer than a church mouse, he doesn't even have a room of his own, if it hadn't been for the carrier just managing to say, amid his panting and groaning, anyone who buys the cupboard will regret it but also anyone who doesn't.

Itching to do it, Ilir secretly counts his money, it should be enough, hands over the amount, surprisingly reasonable, and is no longer alone in the infant morning — the twittering of the sparrows can still be heard — but together with his cupboard, his friend in need. The wood feels wobbly, made in the old days, Ilir grins as he imagines his uncle's reaction, but then he decides that discretion's the better part of valor and lugs the wooden monster into the store, pushing it past the spice jars, behind the desk into the farthest corner and awaits the unpleasant as well as the pleasant surprise the vendor mentioned.

Nothing happens, his uncle chides him, get a hold of that broom, you brat, Ilir sweeps up obediently, dusts and serves the first customers and with the hours, the packets of spice, the lunch break, and his uncle barking orders, he forgets the cupboard, although in the evening, before he locks up, he thinks, I should have done something else with the money, stupid cupboard. In irritation he kicks the cupboard door, spilling black pepper, let Uncle pick it up.

Next morning, when his guilty conscience sends him to his workplace earlier than usual, the peppercorns have been swept up, not one has escaped, also the floor has been wiped and the rooms aired, Ilir can smell the freshness, it can't have been done much earlier, and when his uncle comes in and praises his nephew for the tidiness and cleanliness, your father feels he's been made a fool of. He just did it himself, he thinks querulously, to make me feel ashamed, and Ilir does, in fact, feel ashamed and crawls into the farthest corner, beside the cupboard.

He gives the exterior a half-hearted polish, scratches at it a little and leans against the side, the wood feels warm, almost soft. Then closing time, Ilir shoots off, but the next day he finds that the shop has been wiped down, swept and aired again, again his uncle's pleased and Ilir bewildered, he goes into a corner, but a plan is hatched: he'll stay and watch the store, there's something odd going on here. His uncle's happy with that, the epitome of hard work, he says, can hardly praise him enough and totters off home content. Ilir closes the shop, puts out the light and hides behind the linen cupboard. It's tight, he has to force himself into the gap, hold his breath, but —

a creaking, hardly audible, something is casting a shadow, a lion slinks in through the door, a lion? a mane at least, that's for sure, slinks into the evening atmosphere, past Ilir

76

(alarmed, bewildered, close to a return to childhood when there were still ghosts and monsters) looks around disembodied, all at once extends a pair of shoes, bares two arms and hands, and finally a face —
a girl, small, delicate, starts to tidy up the store; sometimes she lets out a sigh, then it seems to Ilir as if there were no loneliness anywhere else.

It's an hour before your father plucks up the courage to address her, only when her toe collides with a table leg and she emits a human cry does he feel bold enough to ask if she's hurt herself. Struck with fear, she hadn't expected to find anyone in the store, she can't open her mouth, Ilir has to help her, gives her a gentle slap.
She says she's called Emine, she's often seen him, Ilir, in the store, among the pepper and salt, and has fallen in love with him. When her father wanted to marry her off to another man, she just slipped into the cupboard and bribed the carrier to sell her wooden hideout to Ilir; she didn't know what else to do, she says. Ilir finds her rhubarb eyes disconcerting, should he believe her or not? somehow the former seems the safer option, so he nods.
A year later they were married, you say, though I can't believe you because you invent stories, recount fantasies as soon as you open your mouth. Are you following a tradition of your country, using the absurd and impossible, defending dumbbells and maidens in cupboards to make yourself more easily understood, or is the word *realistic* not in your vocabulary? was it not made for you or did you cast it out of your thoughts after a contemptuous glance at it? Your brain is inhabited by the stories of childhood, it's nice for them there, cozy; nonsense nibbles at your voice.

After dinner Luminje wants to go for a walk. We stroll

77

through childhood, walking between six-foot walls, little ramparts: in a labyrinth. The *Minimarket* on the corner has everything you need, coffee, tea, flour, sugar, orange sun blinds and a display window that's too small to display things in.

In the evening the village is taken over by the stray dogs, years ago the KFOR soldiers had to kill whole packs of them because there were too many, in B., where during the war only one person was murdered while in other places whole villages went up in flames, their inhabitants expelled, robbed, tortured, or raped. The victim lived in one of the abandoned houses without roof tiles that stand rather unexpectedly in their gardens, *bisected,* and surrounded by a brick wall, the entrance a traditional Albanian roofed gate, a doorframe with a peaked cap; behind it the village junk yard with spare parts for cars and refrigerators and nearby an *ambeltore* where TORTE, COFFEE EXPRESS, BELSTRA, MAKIATO, and APUCHINO can be bought. The houses in the north with only one too-small window, a bedroom view, why, I ask, Luminje says as a precaution, they're the houses of the Serbs, to stop anyone getting injured if all the windows were smashed, cobblestones have been thrown.

The empty wash line is swinging between the houses, a decorative border with clothes pins, logs for heating and cooking are stacked in the gardens, and on some windowsills there is a handful of garden. The sky is bisected by power cables, the ground by main roads of a dubious nature, and the roofs adorned with the tops of the chimneys, curved, almost in the Chinese style.

A tractor is puttering down the main street, the *hoxha's* singing, some dogs bark along with him, others trot on deserted paths, a pregnant bitch pants her way from one bit of shade to the next, the hair on her belly and back all matted, torn off on her neck and legs, scars and traces of dried blood on her paws. Crows huddle up in cool recesses on the roofs, even the garbage is crouching flat on the ground beside rusty trash cans with burn marks. Satellite dishes, fallen UFOs with their aerials sticking up, are fixed to the balconies. Sheets and underpants would flutter if there were any wind. The villagers, who are preventing the owner from building a house on his own property because they're afraid it might be a brothel, shuffle their way home with their shopping bags —

if they don't happen to be following us: we already have a small procession behind us, only a few take a sniff of foreign culture from their hiding place.

You're not happy with this curiosity, you wish you were far away. With every step we take, more and more villagers follow us, more and more relatives, there's only one uncle who lives elsewhere, in Pristina, and even he's built a house here, for the weekends, he's growing vegetables in the garden like your mother.

I see hardly any ruined, damaged buildings, everything was rebuilt in the very first year after the war, Luminje says, the money's not there for the finishing touches but the most important parts have been there for ages.

A stream winds its way through B., we follow its course, the croaking of the frogs, pass a plot where a father and son have been building a house since the end of the war. There's not much to see yet, only the foundations and a bit of wall, but what it does have is an ideal toilet cubicle, completely tiled with swimming dolphins and a gold doorknob, they should move into the john, Luminje giggles.

We don't miss the cow in the front garden either; it takes up the whole of it, just fitting in between the rose bushes. She's to be pitied, though, has to do without a hat of her own, a

pointed straw hat, you can pick one up in ten minutes, Fehmi says. All the households have given up their guns and yet they reappear, plastic versions for children, how do they sell? I ask, pretty well, your brother says.
Before the war there were thirteen houses, now there are more than three hundred.

A raw egg rolls down between Emine's breasts, smashes on the floor. Lukja nods, content, Nusha laughs up her sleeve, both women are confident that it will be a quick and easy birth but to be quite sure they give your mother water blessed by the *hoxha*, sprinkling it on her breasts and belly. They don't bother with the magic spoons, there seems to be enough magic going on as it is, how ever did she get pregnant, people say the couple had already given up and then, out of the blue, a child, and a son at that, perhaps, only perhaps, people whisper, there's something fishy about the business and there was an exchange, bargaining, then another exchange —
Ilir doesn't care: despite the forty days of abstinence, he grins cheerfully at family and friends, his gun, a rifle, at the ready to greet your arrival.

The infant slides down between Emine's knees into a world of sheepskin surrounded by the female half of the family, already the *hoxha*'s whispering "Luan" in your right ear.
The afterbirth doesn't come out quickly, hot clay is spread on Emine's back and soles. After giving birth she has to have a lot of milk, butter and fatty food so she will recover quickly. She'll stay in bed for three days, on no account must she leave the room, Lukja's convinced that would mean disaster. Your grandmother puts a broom in front of the cradle to keep evil spirits away, hides silver coins between your blankets, and glues a wolf's tooth to your hair with wax, they are to protect you from the evil eye; finally she makes it clear to Nusha that

Emine must never be or sleep in the room alone and at night, at night the light must not go out.

After three days presents and congratulations start to trundle in: *May Luan be noble, hard and tough as an oak tree, and find a wife who is strong enough to continue his clan.* The female relatives gather in the evening, sing and dance, waiting for the third hour to have a look at your future. Turkish coffee is brewed and emptied out, then the cups turned upside down and Nusha, the clairvoyant, interprets the grounds.

She prophesies: you will have many sons, a big house with a vegetable and fruit garden, a dog, two cows, sheep, a flock of hens and three cocks to crow in the morning. You will study in Istanbul, spend your honeymoon in the Caucasus, your hands will be exceptionally slim and long, your body powerful and wiry, and your eyes blue, blue like this night and all the previous nights.

How wrong she was: your hands are podgy and round, your body weak and small, and your eyes black, black as nights should never be at the age of two.

Later I recognize you at a distance from your shambling walk, your silhouette a ridiculously thin braid, mended and fraying at the edges, and when you raise your hand to wave to me, it's a leaf moving, an autumn leaf.

6

What do I associate with Pristina? A town like a through road, *linear, traffic-ridden*, which during the day hides its charm under mountains of garbage, jerry-built houses, only becoming imposing at night, when filling in between the lights is left to the imagination? No, I say, not that.

We're on the sidewalk, *porous*; on the drive to the mortuary in Rahovec, we've made a short detour to the capital, just a quick look, I said, I just wanted to see if anything had changed. Now we're in the *Rruga Nënë Teresa*, the wind's gone and with it the rain, the sun's shining, but despite that the soles of our shoes are whispering at every step, and I say not much has changed since last year, it's still unbearably hot in summer and I can remember hurrying through the streets in a vain search for shade; as if by chance my smile covers up the wrong undertone —

at the end, flight from a locked apartment, balancing on the wall, sparse grass growing on it, an unsoft landing, scratches, bruises, scabs on my hands and knees, *armor full of holes*: that's what I associate with Pristina, an ending.

But where's the beginning? look for the beginning: his sunglasses just on the tip of his nose, Sam, Samuel, peers briefly over the top of his glasses, it makes an impression on me because the glance lasts just a second too long to be harmless, because it has a note of amazement interwoven with piercing cheerfulness. The seat on Sam's right is empty, on his left are my new colleagues, Marie and Peter from Administration, Claude, the photographer, and Marek, the pathologist.

Sam: forensic anthropologist, mostly working in (former) crisis areas, successful, never out of work, Irish to the core, although he had to resort to the dictionary for "Good morning," *Maidin mhaith*, his love for Ireland doesn't go that far, not as far as the language; born and brought up close to the border with Northern Ireland, his elder brother in the Marines, his father a bus driver, but only in the east of England, in Ireland he sleeps in the mobile home, the mobile home behind the clothes line in the garden, his mother a baker, her store a mixture between bakery and tearoom, the wooden teapot by the entrance bright yellow, three purring cats underneath the bird table and around the corner the view of the lough, a black lake, that's what it looks like when, in the summer, I walk along its stony bank, the aromatic rain falling in swift lines.

A view of Sam's sea: it forms sunny folds, still smooth in the morning, fishland, later it rolls in closer, capturing the coast. I'm familiar with it as a soughing from behind the chest of drawers, here it seems in disguise.

A view of Sam's village: the gathering in the pub yawns, oversalted. Outside Sam's house, Ginger, the July cat with flakes of wholemeal in its fur, is purring, under cover. Sheep sleep standing up, the herd of tourists in the woolly valley shivers with cold, it's going to rain —

spent the previous days in the west, on the miniature island, *Inis Óirr,* just big enough to walk round in an afternoon, and it takes forty minutes to the peak, after all it is a mountain. What else is there to do on this raft of an island but sit on the beach, look for a stone which, warm from the meager sunbeams, invites you to sit on it and then doze off wondering whether one can feel the ground of the island gently paddling? Or spend the afternoon, with cider, Guinness and chips at the *hurling,* jumping, inwardly, whenever the opposing player manages to avoid the raised hockey stick, true, he's protected by his helmet and mask, but the extended arm does seem to be out to get heads, and outwardly joining in the *raucous shouts!* when the little white ball flies into the net, it's what's done, anything else would be alien, much too alien.

It's still June; I get the taxi driver to drop me off at the gate of the Psychiatric Institute, my office is three streets farther, they told me, I just need to keep walking straight on, it's a white cube, I can't miss it, I've put my Albanian dictionary away, he speaks German; like many Kosovo Albanians, he's been a *Gastarbeiter* in Germany.

After a few steps along the avenue of chestnut trees, a newspaper stand, pharmacy, and kebab stand along the edge of the street, Marie suddenly appears in the street, waving to me, here Nora, we're here. Morning coffee, breakfast cigarettes, a lethargic conversation about something I don't understand, then, shoulder backpacks and off past mental patients spending a few minutes smoking in the doorway, the only place there's a narrow strip of shade. Marie shows me the office, the hum of the air conditioning interrupted by radio music, otherwise I'm enveloped in a layer of quiet and the distant chug-chug of vehicles on the way to Macedonia. A few minutes later, following Sam's invitation, I'm sitting in his off-road vehicle looking for corpses, maps and typed witness statements in my lap, a truck at our heels laden with shovels, behind it an excavator, as we go a friendly chat about Irish singing competitions, first prize a barrel of beer.

A cross-country trudge, through thistles hidden in the grass, a sly prick in the back, we're heading for the skeleton of a house, the floors caved in, some sloping down into the ground, a two-story building with the beginnings of a third story, *brick-free*, the bricks were stolen, Sam says, three missing persons are said to be buried somewhere around here. He strides across the field in knee-high boots with thick soles, a straw hat, sunglasses and with sunblock on his arms and nose, looking, as he explains, for give-away features, disturbed earth.

He walks up and down the terrain, his eyes fixed on the ground, then he's off with the green excavator and the truck in its train, the policewoman looks for somewhere out of the sun, finds a patch of semi-shade and calls me over, gives me little dark-red cherries to eat, a speciality, she says. They're sour, I bend down to bury the pits, a habit, but the ground won't play ball, it's too hard, the surface sharp, a cutting edge; different shoes next time, the policewoman says, I nod.

The search is unsuccessful, we sit, exhausted, sun-soaked, near the air conditioning; when Sam asks if I'd like to have dinner with him, I say I'd love to. The dull light of the street lamps hardly has any effect on the night sky; the first tiredness is breathing down my neck, voracious, but no place seems right, there are always stones in the way, thistles or plastic bottles, eventually we end up in Sam's apartment. Socks are scattered all over the floor, sockcastles, among them trousers, books, old bars of chocolate, newspapers, CD holders and a box of candy the size of a shoe box, a monstrous bride and groom on the lid.

At the weekend an excursion to Prizren. We do the Sharr mountains, greenery, the colors dazzling after the gray of Pristina, on top of that the forest smell, the rustling of the leaves, at the back the trees grow right up to the town, nestling against burnt-out houses, empty windows, abandoned, the owners dying while fleeing, or should I say on one of the countless times they fled, fleeing from pillar to post, driven away from the first village to the second, from that to a third, only to end up in the first again and to be carted off to the second; before all that, robbed, accused of being terrorists and condemned, stoned or abducted to dig

graves or be draped in the wrong uniforms and used as a human shield in battle —
today there's a piercing twittering, it smells of summer.

Seven years have passed since Fahrie disappeared, six years since you were last in Kosovo, and one year since I was working in Pristina. We are walking on a fraction of the total area of two hundred and eighty-nine square miles, in a city in which, between October 1998 and June 1999, there were countless Serb checkpoints, which the Albanian population avoided as far as possible: checks meant beatings, torture.
Every day megaphones call on them to leave their homeland, better to barricade themselves in even during the day, stack planks of wood. Fear: more and more gun battles, windows smashed, doors demolished, whether Serbian or Albanian makes no difference, bomb attacks on *Minimarkets* and cafés, grenades set off, abductions, arrests, arbitrary and planned, yet it's relatively bearable here, *foreign observers* say, in Pristina, the city that grew at a tremendous rate after the war, even though it is incapable of providing for the hordes of unemployed, on the one hand, overflowing with more than half a million people, on the other, not back to its full population —
fixed with wire to the blue-and-white fence round the OSCE building are the photos of those missing since the end of the war, more than half of them men between their early twenties and forty, the rest women and children, plastic and real dried roses are tied to the wires, above them a placard: TË GJITHËVE NA MUNGOJNË — we miss you all.
The pictures, laminated in plastic with names underneath, have been blighted by the weather, some are unrecognizable by now, especially the faces, eyes, nose, and mouth, seem particularly susceptible to invisibility, in others it's the body, neck, and shoulders, and then the face is left hanging in the

air on the sheet alone; on one the tie is all that's still to be seen, on the next the rain and dirt have made short work of the person portrayed, while others are as clear as if they'd disappeared only recently, only yesterday.

Unconsciously I equate the condition of the picture with the time since the person has disappeared, has been missed, instinctively I also equate the intensity of the pain with the sharpness of the image, their chance of being found with the shininess of the photo. Life or death, being found or not being found, tied to the quality of photographic paper.

That's unfair: on a closer look I see that some families have provided an old color photo of the victim; one from the past that can never match the quality of a more recent picture.

Another impression comes to mind: it could just as well be a missing poster for a lost pet, the sense of loss now only marginal, which explains the old, ratty picture. If he should return and see his photo on the fence, would the missing person feel hurt if it wasn't a good picture? Would he say, "Why didn't you use that picture of me at sunset, in the room flooded with dark-yellow light, a light that conceals my weak points?" The idea behind these photos can't be that the missing person himself might walk past the fence, recognize himself and say, "Oh, that's me, I really ought to contact my family," though no possibility should be ruled out.

Perhaps it's easier to mourn nice-looking people than ugly ones, perhaps the brain needs beauty to balance out the feeling of emptiness, of pain? After all, wouldn't it be hurtful to display a poor photo of someone, even if that person doesn't exist anymore? On the other hand, you object, would anyone put up a photo of a missing relative at a place that has nothing to do with their biography if one believed that person would come back? Looked at from that point of view, you say, these people are those who have already been given up by their families, people who are as faded as their portraits, the portrait gallery merely serves as a memorial, *nothing more* —

and you start to feel that the right thing to do is to get on with your life instead of mourning the past, letting yourself be put in deep freeze, shutting yourself off from any future, even if passively, even if it's you who *are being* shut off from any future, and yet you feel it's wrong to give up without any news, cruel, as if it were murder —

and suddenly you understand, in the shade it becomes clear to you that you're not the only one, that the faces on this stretch of the street have relatives who have been through the same as you, and you start to ask yourself whether it would really be simpler to hide in a foreign country, lock your grief away, keep it to yourself, come with time to believe it hit you alone worst of all. What do you know of the war, all those years you thought, from a safe distance, that you had avoided it successfully —

and I keep staring fixedly at the sidewalk, afraid you'll start to speak as soon as our eyes meet but, crustacean that you are, you don't notice much in your shell apart from the wind turning.

We're walking across grass, the university gardens, to the library, which consists of countless little cubes with railings around them, the roofs white spheres cut in half, *plisi*, past the statue of Mother Teresa and child in the dried-out fountain and the memorial to Gjergj Kastrioti Skënderbeu, an Albanian national hero from the fifteenth century, initially a hostage to the sultan to whom his father had had to submit, later a military commander for and defier of the Ottoman Empire, and that for twenty-five years, especially heroic, on horseback, with sword, beard and pointed hat, outside the brand-new, glittering government building.

We walk past the Kosovo Museum and the Fatih Mosque, which managed to avoid the fate of being used as a toilet, which befell most of the Orthodox churches, at least those that weren't torched or torn down; we go to see the city center, where we sit under one of the many sunshades in the garden of the Grand Hotel Pristina: the scene of many demonstrations of tens of thousands of Albanians against the Serbian government before the war and the *sub-center* for torture and interrogation by the Serbian police, the *main center* being the infamous Police Station No. 92. Later the hotel was one of the two places where Albanian Kosovans had to go to register, after being questioned about possible membership of the UÇK, in order to get a *Green Card,* which was to indicate that they were *legitimate* inhabitants; people who didn't have such a card were deported, maltreated en route to being deported, locked up, and only freed on payment of between five hundred and a thousand German marks. Now it's the meeting place for all those who don't know Pristina, people are always waiting outside the hotel entrance; in addition, two hundred agents of the *Albanian Secret Service* are said to have been observed in the hotel foyer.

A smoker's paradise: to sit comfortably, puffing away, while teenagers try to sell cigarettes, imitations of well-known brands. Everything is imitation, you say, Kosova imitation paradise, and decline them. At the next table an American tourist, early twenties, no shorts, but trainers and enthusiasm: Bill Clinton's everywhere over here, he says, there's a Bill Clinton Avenue, Bill Clinton restaurants, not forgetting the big poster of Clinton with *Welcome to Pristina* on it; as an American, he says, I've never felt so much at home on any of my travels.
In the streets white UN buses with plastic windows, *catapult-proof,* transport for the few Serbs remaining in Kosovo, every

89

day you see fewer and fewer of them driving around; also military-green KFOR off-road vehicles with national flags, little obstacles on the slalom course of the legless man who heaves himself over the crossing on his way to the winding streets of the residential area where the VW buses with eight seats and the little square signs with their number between the windshield wipers are less frequent, feeble competition for the big, *proper* buses, old tourist buses which never move with their doors closed and are gifts from European firms, or a convenient method of waste disposal? What other explanation is there for the odd inscriptions? on bus no.10 it says *Oltner Tagblatt*.

Keep on living at all cost, you say, we're so desperate to function that we forget everything else.

Pristina, a city that is not a city: no city center, just two main streets that cross in the middle of the town. The dominant shape: cuboid. The dominant color: browny beige. A superfluity of sunlight. Shade has to be created by the inhabitants themselves, they are all seekers after shade, their holy grail: sunshades. The dominant noise: the roar of trucks, heavy wheels rolling over streets, the creak of construction work, building materials being raised and lowered, welding, boring, mixing concrete, engines idling, electricity generators chugging, there are still frequent power failures, especially in winter; Albanian pop music from the loudspeakers of the little CD stands along the main street to dam up our taciturnity, the clatter of coffee cups in the countless overfull cafés or *pasticerias* and, of course, the buzzing of the flies during the day, only audible when there's silence.

Like mushrooms, satellite dishes sprout one after another from window boxes and projecting balconies. Bungalows like Frankenstein's monster, their masonry plundered from several different houses, the roof from their neighbor, the façade from the abandoned house next door, and the entrance hall, which serves as wardrobe, winter garden, and toolshed, put together out of blue raincoats and plastic tablecloths.

Everywhere washing is fluttering on the line. Children play at hopscotch on the sidewalk, slide down bicycle ramps, beggars hang head down in garbage containers, people look on them dully as they reemerge. Streets are given a daily bath, dust prevention. In places different grass grows: rubbish. The chirping of birds, in two parts, just as persistent as the roar of engines, the crunch of wheels on asphalt. Potholes, up to three feet deep, temporally filled with empty beer cans, packets, leftover food and newspapers. In the evening damp, related to early dew, people walk straight down from one end of the main street to the other, then back again, they don't stroll in loops.

Everywhere *Kina Shops*, everywhere bridal stores, one display dummy beside the next, with permanent waves. The market ends in stands: CD stands, sunglass stands, perfume stands. By the entrance a man selling wooden spoons is dozing: short white hair, white mustache, *plisi* on a floral cushion on his knee, leaning against his backpack, his sunshade full of holes, his bare arms and feet red. Outside the market fortress, stranded *garbage whales*.

The continuing presence of the war -- I. Stamped or written: JO NEGOCIATA — VETËVENDOSJE!/ we don't negotiate, we want to decide ourselves; and on posters: BOJKOTONI PRODUKTET E SERBISE/ boycott products from Serbia. UN building, UN automobiles, the white spots in the cityscape. *Elektro-Böhme* strayed here from Bad Tennstedt. The baroque Austrian post office beside the mosque attracted no acts of aggression.

The continuing presence of the war – II. Stamped or written:

12:44 TIME'S UP — UNMIK GO HOME. Unbroken windows indicate a house is inhabited.

An unfinished city: people are happy to sit on projecting walls, later these will be transformed into balconies with children, parents, and outstretched legs, well-aired toes. I walk along, eyes down, I feel looked at, as if people were trying to make me disappear by constant staring; many foreigners are working here, *Internationals*, who, however, have lost a lot of their popularity since their arrival after the war, only yesterday there was a brawl in a bar — *Pristina, Partyzone!* — locals versus non-locals, they earn more than three times as much for the same work, we can't afford it, your brother says, dependence is too expensive, independence on the other hand —

A detour down a side street, a narrow, unpaved alleyway, almost a village street with a view of the rear of the high-rise buildings, the first two stories blocked out by little bungalows squatting beside bushes, between them peaceful garbage sit-ins, their window panes replaced by paper, in the window boxes clumps of tomatoes, pigeons swinging on the power lines. One front garden is an antique store, the carpets rolled up, stacked, the pictures and bedposts wrapped in green cloth, and this lonely alley with puddles from the rain two days ago, with the faded house number 12 on ocher plaster, the venetian blinds let down to its chin, and above the tiled roofs grey high-rise blocks, *mountains*, if you like, is as quiet as nowhere else in Pristina; there seems to be no past here.

You stop at a notice announcing someone's death, attached by four thumb tacks to a tree, the bark's reserved for that purpose, beside the picture of the dead man is his name and the word *njoftim*, announcement, below it the time and place of the funeral. You can get them with green, red, or black

edging, you say; Islam prefers green, the older generation of males red, in homage to Tito. These notices don't just keep to trees, they're also stuck on lamp poles and advertising columns, but trees, you say, are the best place —
why not announce death on plants? and then if one day you're not sure which of your friends is still alive, you'll go for a walk round the city center looking for the death trees and reading their messages.

On the edge of the city: tin shacks with piles of tires and wrecked cars, *Auto Servis*. Plastic floral wreaths for war heroes, extra long-lasting. In the sunshine it smells erroneously like shade.
We drive via Fushë Kosovë and Malishevë, past dried-up, blackened corn and abandoned fields; if it wasn't for the neighboring fields, I would assume they were natural meadows. Another stray dog, coat all tattered, prowling past warning signs about mines this time, *Mina* is written on them, white on red.
The ruined houses look more inhabited than the *fresh* ones, each with its grow-your-own vegetable garden. In some places grass is still cut with scythes. We drive past motels, transfer points for human trafficking, you don't say anymore. At regular intervals we see round yellow signs with a black dog, the KFOR signs, the dog the symbol for Pristina.
Graveyards in nowhere. A generally luxuriant sky, fluffy clouds. Cocks crow at night as well.

There is a superabundance of time here; a new idea, not having to economize —
you say, in two hours we'll be in Rahovec.

Present absent ones, their presence unbearably lasting, basically the nature of this existence consists of presence despite absence — or precisely because of absence, absence always determined by presence — and yet this presence is of greater durability than the absence brought about by short separations; being dead is being absent.

Even if, years later, memory starts to fade, it is kept alive with rituals — lighting candles, going to the cemetery: as if the graves were homes and the cemetery an address, according to the logic of the living, perhaps, existing without a home an impossibility, without belonging, without identity, it is only by belonging to a grave that a dead person acquires the greater part of their identity.

The dead also live, and they keep on dying, again and again, for them being alive is a constant fluctuation between death and life, now they are back in their childhood, now in adolescence, always with that little unspoken appendage after and between the sentences: their status as dead in the here and now.

Going through light barriers in reverse, pointless, the silence a wall, a giant wall, communication broken off to excess, a rage of silence, a rage of raging silence, every corpse making a mockery of speech, unbearable the quiet that seems to attach itself to every farewell, or is it perhaps showing solidarity with the silence of the corpses, a dialogue of the dead as one starts to remain silent on one's own part, as if the one who remains silent were a person speaking *Deadish*, a dialect of the general, harmless Silence; but those who do not speak this dialect are condemned to swing back and forward between the places of speaking and of remaining silent, constantly paddling from one bank to the other, lingering, settling is not allowed, there is something driving them on — dying is a habit, a bad habit, would it were possible to cast it off or to cast it onto others, the others who are even allowed to pass away, no matter, and those who may have managed to evade the custom, who may have found an anti-mortality patch, would not be to blame for the billions of dead who didn't have one because it didn't even occur to them to look for one; but perhaps they succumbed to their addiction.

(And how is it that it spreads, how is it that death spreads, how is it that people die in little groups, like parakeets? So that later on, after one has given up the bad habit, one can decompose in little piles?)

Rescuing creates scars, that's the way Sam sees it, rescuing the corpses from the bottom of the pit, he calls it *rescuing*, for him exhumation is recovering, some see it as sinful, desecration, after all, during the examination he will snip away at them, saw off parts of the body that may have been discolored by the effects of weather or storage and, by putting the human remains together, create a completeness which, in its bareboned nakedness, ought to make us ashamed, not to mention the stench of the corpses; they worm their way into our memory, gases given off by putrefaction —

humans as things, human things after the metamorphosis, have no insides, contain nothing, conceal nothing, are entirely subsumed in their surface and at every moment are exactly what they appear to be; the way Sam sees it, they only have one story to tell, the story of dying.

An interpreter, at the same time a translator, is how he describes his function, and when, pencil behind his ear and wearing breathing mask and protective clothing, he bends over the body parts, horror only creeps over him to a limited extent, even if more and more as time passes; in the

95

beginning, Sam says, it was still enthusiasm, euphoria, excitement, which only expressed itself in bated breath but not in trembling hands, then it crept over him, gradually, the sickness that is death, the bad *habit*, and Sam started to see cadavers everywhere, above all when he was sleeping, body parts in his dreams, and in broad daylight, even shutting, locking himself in didn't help, they slip through the walls, as we know —

rescuing creates scars, there are particular models of them: nightmares plague the majority of the rescuers, Sam and his colleagues, his friends, his *family*, because that's what they are, family; they spend day and night, days and nights together, they're well beyond the Darby and Joan stage. They are more than just a unit, constantly exchanging things, music, books, toothpaste, shower gel, clothes, they only possess the basic essentials, their backpacks their permanent residence. And then the experience of death, it welds people together, Sam says, we compare the *infection* of death, observe it spreading inside us and eventually only exist as strangers in our own body, which it seems impossible to feel unless we keep at least a little distance between ourselves and death by closing our eyes to the surrounding circumstances; no witness statements while we're working on mass graves, no additional information, the grave and the corpse are sufficient.

We need distance, Sam says, because otherwise we'd be forced to empathize with the victims, because we'd identify with them, because we'd be incapable of seeing the remains as a puzzle that it's our job to solve; and when I say, "we need distance," *I mean we can't manage without it.*

The first time in the mortuary in Rahovec: several containers stuck together, guarded by police, valuable human material, we enter in single file through a narrow, white disinfection sluice, take off our backpacks in a larger room with computers and a dining table for six, sandwiches, then on through the sluice to Container 4, here, men and women individually, in white protective suits, disposable suits, XL size, snowman dress in trash-can material, *rustle-soft*. On one of the three dissecting tables with washbasin and drain, Sam fishes human remains out of a black body bag, numbered on the breast side, the corpse was in water with trousers, shirt and socks on, they form a skin where there's none left and I have to swallow, I find it impossible to see the everyday aspect of this situation, and yet everything's so *normal*, a matter of such unbearable routine, that my back turns to jelly and my knees give way. They take me to the cloakroom, as if I'd feel more at home in that laying battery, surrounded by dark wood.

To the crackle of sausages during the lunch break, Marek, who always speaks to the Albanians in Serbian, *after all, they learned it at school!* decides to have a glass of wine and another and another, laughs, legs wide apart, at jeans, jeans, he says, kids' clothes, and drags us off to the winery, it's right next door, and since we're here, a guided tour please, down the steps, down down down to the first and second floor, past oaken barrels, they're giants, squashed planets. It's cool, damp, the melodious plash of drips over the soft murmur of the wind through chinks in the door, gaps in the window, we'd like to stay, Sam, Marek, and I, we'd like never to leave —
it's so easy to fall silent, swallowed up like that.

Dealing with corpses an outrage: not only not being allowed to be an observer, but exchanging civilities with the dead person, extracting samples; on the other hand, we could never just observe, death as an exhibit would be unbearable for us, Sam says. Robbed of all individuality, the corpse, the *resistor*, consists of death, but also of humanity, a strange mixture which doesn't look good, neither on an empty stomach nor on full eyes; even identification only helps to a limited degree, in fact, hardly helps at all, for it is only family photos that make the full extent of deadness discernible, certainty, yes, a dead certainty.

To me it seems almost pointless, I hardly dare say it out loud, to want to identify an assemblage of bones, not a human being, but also not an object, something halfway between, sightless, skinless, soulless, limited similarity to roots, branches, or a grandfather's staff; does a corpse have identity? do body parts have identity? that's a contradiction, death means the complete loss of identity, these questions force themselves on me, whirl around and around above my head, I stuff them back in my mouth —

just don't fall out.

(Or does the manner of our death say something about us?)

How little similarity, how devastatingly small the similarity between the living person and the corpse, and here we're not talking about bones but about the whole cadaver, about a freshly dead body, to bend over it, to kiss it farewell, unthinkable, healthy defense mechanism, is death not the most healthy thing that can happen?

While they're mopping up in the next room, summer heat already in April, tongue twisters without end, in July it will thaw, the *tongue of ice*, the corpse is both present and absent at the same time, its gaze is not fixed on the same world. Perhaps, though, it's the living who are absent for the dead, absent present ones, perhaps it's the exact opposite, which explains the parallel gaze, the misrouted connection; how alive can one be for the dead in order to be considered alive?

Stating the obvious, let's tell it how it is: a corpse is inhuman, how else can one describe this complete lack of behavior, except of course as impolite, unnatural, offensive, asocial, insensitive, a monster in human form, but with what is human about it in the process of disintegration, therefore a being that is gradually reducing its humanity, a thing, assuming thing is the opposite of human being, whose humanity is running out, nonsense, what's all this talk about humanity, humanness is what it is, humanness as far as it relates to the form.

Then jealousy creeps in, no, envy, envy of the thing in a human form that's close to its expiry date, this incredible independence of everything, food, place, beyond desire, happy since absolutely free —

the freedom the void allows. The corpse is a hollow creature.

(Brief guide for freedom fighters: in order to achieve freedom, one has to learn how to die, to practice a corpse existence.)

His compulsion to polish shoe boxes, dry out scraps of paper if stray rain should happen to come in through the window — superstition. Sam the hermit, committed to putting a stop to evil although he is slowly losing his belief that he is actually managing to prevent further murders, that he can change, improve the world bit by bit, more than a belief, his mission in life; now, twenty years later, his perspective has changed, his mission is in decline, and a worm's eye view? An impossibility.

Constantly poking around in the past, a telephone call's enough to make you lose your appetite, and then the daily chatter, the murmur of voices outside the window, rush hour in the streets, the chirping of the birds in the courtyard, the daily chatter shrill, unbearably loud, your ears aren't used to it anymore, they're tuned in to the language of the dead, to their silence. The past is mute, it expresses itself in images, not sentences, in quiet places; a sigh is the most powerful verbal expression of the past.

Thus with time Sam runs out of language, it empties itself with every bone he examines, a gradual but constant development, empties itself with every leg he examines, every arm, with all the phalanges that look like pebbles; he realizes it himself with regret, panic — how uncivilized he might seem — but also with relief, it appears that too many words make contact with the present absent ones more difficult, thoughts, mental blockages, associations form, and with the blockages, the associations, the chains of images peppered with words, sentences, exclamation marks, feelings arise. They penetrate his shield and he grieves, despite his protective clothing —

Grieving a *sickness*: impossible to carry on working, the dead body no longer an object of analysis but a human being. In its in-between state the corpse assumes the mask of the person, gives itself the air of identity and its personality, previously invisible, appears, as if from nowhere.

I'm allowed to be there when they do the x-rays, in the little chamber next to the autopsy room, the entrance covered by heavy cloth; I'm wearing a lead vest, armor, speckled — with blood? — a body is on the black table, it's come from the refrigerated container in the yard, the oversized, light gray construction-site toilets. Slowly Sam's assistant passes the lens of the x-ray over the remains, there's the bullet, he says, pointing at the screen, the surface with black and white precipitation, a snowstorm, frozen for the blink of an eye, a standstill, I can't see anything, only an arctic landscape. He circles the cartridge on the x-ray print-out, hands it to me, thin, shiny paper, and sends me to Sam, I find him at the dissecting table. The scent of lemon from a bottle hangs in the air, but there is a stronger smell of damp soil, not flowerpot soil from the balcony, a homey garden plot, but remoistened earth, dried mud; in one corner a plastic skeleton, on the walls orange pipes and curling, dog-eared sheets of paper, tables to help determine age and sex, one third of identity.

I look over Sam's shoulder, what're you doing there? Help me find any fractures, Sam says, with fractures you're halfway to a name. Are those the names he murmurs in his sleep, or is he defending himself against the ones who have remained anonymous, the masses in the grave? From his tone of voice, I'd say Sam is justifying himself, to the dead, to their relatives, as he rolls over, breathes in deeply, as if he'd done too little, said too little, woe betide him if he blurts out names. We drink tea and wait, wait, wait, time is short, it's always too short, make more of it, he's tempted to say, and give me some of it, a few scraps will suffice —

to stick bones together, reconstruct skulls, speed up the drying process with a hair dryer or sun-warm air, find anatomically correct positions, clean up pelvises, the tips of ribs, collarbones, they tell you the age of the corpse, the length of the thigh bone its height, the teeth perhaps its family. And then to photograph parts of the skeleton so that its death will not be unatoned. So it's all about revenge? I ask. I don't know, Sam says, a standard response, a variable, which is used for many answers, but which always means the same: *I've lost my ability to think.* Hardly surprising when death has contaminated his bedroom; in dreamland, the realm of the dead, he sometimes comes across cases, his cases, dead people or even just parts of dead people, it doesn't make any difference whether they float up to him whole or cut up in pieces and while its happening it doesn't strike him, later, after he's woken up, he racks his brains, I felt I knew them so well, but where did we meet? only on the dissection table are they classified, recognized, as if he's always known that *person.*

But chosen ones do not give up: he feels he's been chosen, his work is more than just work, it is work that makes sense of things, living work, since it will live on after him and his colleagues. The earth is full of dead people, that's the way

Sam sees it when he goes for a walk on deserted ground, the earth lodgings of a different kind: a temporary store.

What Sam doesn't know: we're rewinding; night is already falling, a stray dog howls outside the window, the light in the bedroom's not worked for weeks. I switch on the terrace light and see, my eyes close up against the glass, layers of dried rain; I creak open wardrobe doors, pull blouses, skirts, trousers off the hangers, I take everything, my disappearance is to be noticeable, arouse curiosity, I roll everything up, deposit it in my backpack with a backward glance, pointless, that's his evening call, he'll be two hours late.
I outwit the locked apartment by climbing out of the window onto the terrace and over the fence, I had to let myself be locked in, we only have one key, I go to the phone booth, order a taxi, run back, wait with my bag by the front door, then off to the airport, the plane's late, suddenly my name from the loudspeaker, has Sam found me already? No, my plane's delayed —

Visible until just a few days ago, all at once I'm invisible, I don't exist anymore, even though there's still me in the form of a body; I exist in neither thought nor feeling, I'm hardly even a presence: today I'm just a disembodied voice. Too late I noticed the expiration date, the *small-speak*, underneath his vows. Absent, not present, only of value as a missing person, I think, then the meter would be reset to zero, the expiration date banished to the future and then I could do something about the invisibility, that darned invisibility —
I wait.
My plan doesn't work out, I never hear from Sam again. No words scribbled on a piece of paper or stammered over the telephone. *As if I'd never existed.* Things stayed silent between us, just as silent as now, as we face each other, after a year.

Presently absent, Sam's absence unbearably long lasting, basically a presence that consists of absence, it runs through from Rwanda to Bosnia-Herzegovina, from Bosnia to Kosovo, in between to Ireland, the past, childhood, possibly a future; to experience the present a luxury, for he's accustomed to keeping it out of his mind, examining the corpses takes place separately from his person in a timeless space between past and future, the distance is necessary for survival, to talk about feelings, his own as well as others', is detrimental to survival, the admission of guilt: "I've said too much," follows immediately; his exhumation work excludes humanity.

This superhumanity is binding, a binding commitment to truth and to justice: as a superhuman it ought to be possible to prevent further murders, for death exposed as murder seems avoidable, *as murderers we are saved!* And that is what it's all about, it's a political act to interfere with putrefaction, to bring time to a halt, it's so many things but above all it's rummaging through filth which is difficult to wash off afterwards, the stench of decaying flesh is persistent, soaks through your overall directly into your skin. Our all too mortal mortality can be halted, objections can be raised, we are in a position to correct nature, human *nature*, avoidable death. To save human lives before these lives even exist, the idea doesn't let go, it's more than just a search for justice. It's a great life in the *paradise of the future* —

reemerging in the here and now, on the other hand, is painful, although initially a relief to be back in normal life again, TV, warm water round the clock and not just when it happens to have been raining that day or the neighbors have forgotten to water the vegetable patch; supermarkets where the immense range of goods offered is already starting to torment you, despair revolving around the weekend weather, but after only a few hours this excessive affluence becomes an obscenity, at first illusory, an unreal toy world; a furtive glance between the folds in the clothes of the man sitting next to you in the subway, no, there's not another layer, just the one, he doesn't need to wear two shirts, one on top of the other, two pairs of underpants, he's not fleeing the war, suddenly this revelation throws Sam off balance and he starts wondering seriously where, where on earth, where he actually is. The discovery of the unreality of this existence makes him an outsider in the present, an enemy of his earlier life that has suddenly stopped existing; the return to the familiar has become a pilgrimage to an alien world.

Sam greets me, aware that he deserves an explanation. I greet Sam, aware that I've hurt him, even though his profession makes him better at dealing with people who are absent than with those who are present. We both prefer to remain silent —
to make our impotence at home in speech.
A sunset in the neon light, opening the windows strictly forbidden, requires the exercise of authority. The dictatorship of air conditioning.

It's as if what we remembered wasn't memories, never had been memories, as if there hadn't been any interval in between, as if there were no more than one night between the past meeting and the present one; just for a moment a suggestion of coming close, starting up again, then I remember, a journey into the past, its futility; what a waste of time! An echoing exclamation, with time the exclamation marks increase, what can one do with a corpse-exhumer who spends his time rummaging around in other people's clothes looking for purses, ID-card holders, papers, concealed clues to identity, to *being human,* who spends days on end doing nothing but digging soil out of holes with his bare hands and

who cries on his pillow at night but uses bits of paper handkerchief so as to leave no traces, whose motto is *finality is unacceptable*, and who has a terrible aversion to questions, *questions are taboo*, because they demand answers and his attempt to answer them was bound to fail, even though he let them sniff at him the whole night through, one persistent one above all: *Could that happen to me as well?* No civilities till after my shower, please, what a waste! And the next day an argument, his declaration of war: *The dead are always more important than the living.*
I push you forward, this is Luan Alushi, it's for him that we're here.

A concealed side room, empty apart from a gray table long and wide enough for a coffin of medium-brown wood with a reddish tinge, black at the edges and corners, a bit of cloth is hanging out, Sam pushes it back in through the gap. Elaborate brass decoration at the head and foot, feathers and leaves. Cold air whirring out of the air conditioning.
Beforehand Sam walked up and down in the storage shed, along the stacks of empty coffins — they're handed out with the corpses, a present — between the body bags on the floor, perhaps twenty, perhaps thirty, *don't worry, there's plenty more*, along passageways just a foot wide, looking for Fahrie; from the guard room by the entrance, television froth, the twitter of a soap opera.
It's through the dead that we're connected to their relatives, he recalls having once told me. With our work we can enter the lives of those people and change them by exchanging their memories. You call that helping? was my response, you're not even house trained but obsessed with showing things, and you trample all over other people's grief, what do you mean, *without spattering their soul,* leaving behind an explosion of blotches and images —

I buttoned my lip too late.

Sam starts to explain where they found Fahrie's body and how they identified it, the questionnaire the family filled in, comparison with a DNA sample from her sister. He talks about examining the bones, the jaw, the comparison with breaks from childhood, identity is correspondence, correspondence with the *beforehand* of memory, which feels the urge to cheat when there are gaps, to fill empty spaces, incompleteness being unbearable.

He allows you a quick glance at the corpse, though he advises against it. You ask for the coffin lid to be taken off.

The parts of her body have been placed in the correct position, the skull reconstructed, the joins neatly stuck together —

doing justice to the dead, always; giving them humanity, dignity, that's what Sam calls it, though what he means is an appearance of humanness. Freeing the bodies from the ground, they ended up in that place against their will, it's an error that must be corrected, homeless human remains, their arbitrariness offensive. And yet there are family members who prefer them not to dig for their missing ones, that's only for the dead, but missing persons are alive, the first shovelful of earth an act of betrayal. So the family doesn't want their missing member back, Sam asks, in whatever condition? Ignorance is bliss.

(I can understand their unwillingness to confront it, he thinks, I feel like that from time to time myself, I'm often reluctant to examine a corpse in the harsh light of the dissecting table, in the lab it's a foreign body, the grave its natural environment. There it's so unremarkable that people don't see it unless they're used to *understanding* corpses.)

Away from Rahovec it's deathly quiet. It seems more sensible

to say nothing, it always seems more sensible to say nothing, less awkward? Words can never be found; withdrawn in their shells they even refuse to join in a game of hide and seek, at the end of which they would inevitably be forced to appear. What can one say when faced with a man who insists on seeing his wife one last time, an incomplete skeleton, a broken, patched-up skull, yellowing bones, with a slight smell of decay over it all; what, when you hand him the objects found beside the body, her ID card, a chain, some clothing, which, more real than the body itself, seem to say: *I am dead, I am never coming back*; what when he succumbs to grief, starts to cry —
his tears would be an invitation to speak.

Is it her or is it not her?
Stupid to try and read features into the skull, futile. How much identity can a corpse have, it's nothing but the last remains indicating the departed human being, a negative print. As the past of the person in the present, it's also a piece of timelessness, no, not timelessness but something outside the general rhythm of time, something that makes the clock go more slowly. It's for that reason that all the examining, sawing, extracting cannot affect it, a corpse has no intentions, it could just as well not exist, it has no goal to achieve, it's a leftover.
The answer has to be: *Of course that isn't Fahrie*, and yet it seems to you that it is, but that doesn't make the damaged "we" whole again, on the contrary, one image replaces another, the blurred image of the abduction the needle-sharp one of dissolution. What do you mean, *At one with her after death*, she went long ago, all that's left is her skeleton —
which repels you. Perhaps, like the families before you, you should have screamed, wept, fainted, looked for the perpetrator, found the perpetrator, with violence if necessary,

107

but you walk away —
your steps thin, your face smooth.

You wait outside the door, a torpid afternoon, the distant view an abandoned field. You're standing in the parking lot, one could believe you were enjoying the view, in one hand the death certificate, in the other the bag with Fahrie's clothes. You don't notice us, don't feel you're being observed, certainty has caught up with you, a conclusion but no closure. Sam puts his hand on your shoulder, a cold hand which never really warms up. When you speak, you bruise the silence that has come over us. You ask, *What happened?*

A hundred and fifty yards downstream in G., a village forty-five miles to the east of Pristina, a grave was found beside a bridge, covered with branches and grass, but so shallow that the tips of fingers were sticking out of the ground. Eighteen corpses were exhumed at that spot, two of them female. The examination revealed that the majority of the group had been killed by shots to the head and chest, some beaten to death. The assumption is that they were taken while fleeing and executed.

8

On the edges of uncertain being, I'm *on the edges of uncertain being,*
both feet on the bank but my head leaning over the edge of
the pit, as if it were worth seeing —
the freshly dug grave, a few shovels and planks are lying on
the ground, the shovels rusted, the planks an immaculate
white.
I wasn't allowed to go with you in the mosque, it's not right
for me as a woman to be in the graveyard either, but I asked
if I could and the family allowed me to; you allowed me to.

There's never enough time to learn how to depart this life; is
it unfriendly towards death, a lack of hospitality, or is it dying
that acquires by subterfuge the confidence to strike
unexpectedly?
Even when dying is visible, takes place within visibility,
decline could not be clearer, death would be a relief — it only
seems invisible, in reality it's expelled, outlawed as long as one
feels alive, *young* — it's already too late to learn. Anyway, what
is there to study? to know by heart what it's like to die, would
that lessen the fear? would a vacation course *How to die well* do
that? While we're dying, our soul creeps up into our throat,
you repeat childhood memories, fragments of stories your
grandparents told, death flows into our body, then, after forty
days, the angel of death, Izrâ'il, takes our soul.
Izriâ'il, the angel with four faces, of which one is floating
under the soles of his feet, another behind his back, held on a
cord, whose body consists entirely of tongues and eyes, and
who has seventy thousand feet and forty thousand wings
which stretch from the earth up to heaven, from the
easternmost to the westernmost point, the whole world in his
hands with all its mountains, valleys, rivers, forests, turnpikes,

skyscrapers, airports, a winged giant with sparse hair, a thick beard, a bulbous nose, and eyebrows that are so bushy that they cast immense shadows, shadows the size of a whole night.

But then you think you've heard that people who are dying are visited by four angels, luminous beings, not hobgoblins with wings; the first sucks the soul out of the right foot, the second out of the left foot, the third out of the right and the fourth out of the left hand. At first those who are dying are able to speak and use the opportunity to tell of the beings that are made of the same material as souls, but gradually their tongues resist the words and they fall silent as the last bit of their soul slips out through the tips of their fingers.

A good soul glides out of the body, you say, but a bad one lets go unwillingly, clinging with all its might to its previous residence with its littlest fingers, even with its teeth; it growls and doesn't let go, a little *bee*; not a bee, your grandmother interjects, the soul is a human being the size of bee. When an angel has finally caught it, it sits, trembling, on the palm of his hand —

a drop that's been given a nudge.

She didn't die the way one ought to, you say, Fahrie didn't die the way one ought to, or was her death meant to be more abrupt than any other? Even if her death, *if you think about it properly*, was drawn out, even if she seemed to die a little more every day, she was untraceable, as if being missing were a terminal disease but one which still left the hope that she would recover, that her presence would be able to assert itself *against all reason;* you waited in order to avoid the farewell, not to find out that it is unavoidable.

She didn't die the way one ought to, the words come out during the burial, while the coffin is being lowered into the pit, the planks laid like a tent over the coffin lid, and the first mourners starting to fill in the grave. It was winding up inside you, *winding up*, and that *anger*, that unbearable anger, welled up, a different face, one it would be undesirable to see; now, with the words pouring out, you *flail* at them, at their shoveling, digging, filling in, the silence is broken, the drought was cracking anyway. Your *flock of words* comes out in painful contractions, you're speaking to cover up your fear and the *afterwards*; you're speaking against death, angrily, it would be impossible for you to remain silent, painful; only by speaking do you think you can feel the standstill of time, a *far-off place*; your speaking embarrasses the gathering, they shovel faster, place the railings round Fahrie's grave, a green iron fence as if there were a danger of her escaping, and you, inconsolable, continue to speak —

the grave, an underground cavern, welcomes the good souls. It promises to broaden out, to outwit the narrowness and open a window to paradise. But it warns the bad souls that it's a dark, lonely place inhabited by worms, beetles, maggots. Before life in the grave begins, a journey takes place, a journey to one's future destiny: white angels with rays of light instead of faces, *white holes*, bring a cover from the paradise garden shed, from the old wooden hut with paint that started to flake off when it was only a day old, after you'd found it in the building supply store and trundled it home in a stolen shopping cart on unmade roads through two towns — a cover made of gossamer cloth soaked in musk. They pack up the soul in it and fly through the seven layers of heaven, a swarm of locusts. Bad souls, however, are taken by Izriâ'il down to the guards of hell, and any attempt to reach even the first of the seven heavens is doomed to failure.

Afterwards, you whisper, the soul is sent back to its grave, fearsome angels want to interrogate it. They have claws, flashes of green lightning in their eyes, and thunderous

111

voices. The soul is so afraid that it retreats into its body through a nostril, transforming the corpse for a moment into a sleeper. If in one's former life one was dishonest, malevolent, spiteful, the grave will go up in flames and a window to hell will open, where snakes, scorpions, and spiders wriggle and squirm, where caldrons of water are bubbling, in the background the constant rattle of chains. Evil deeds will turn into dogs and pigs which will chase the common souls, beat, bite, scratch them, the *hoxha* interrupts, *më falni*, excuse me —

For the prayer, spoken in Arabic, we squat down on the burial ground, bend our arms at the elbow, hold the palms of our hands up to the sky and bow our heads. The *hoxha* says an angel will receive Fahrie, she has nothing to fear if she is free from guilt, if that is not the case, then God help her; his voice in a *duet* with your looks, *a dotted rhythm*. You break in, furious, her soul left the earth ages ago, *she died seven years ago*, seven years! Seven years ago her soul circled round your house, watched it from a distance for a month, watched your family slowly build it up again, your mother sewing curtains, your sister painting the walls, your brother fitting new windows, then returned to her grave to see who visited it, who not, who was mourning her, who not. She waited in vain, you say, *she waited in vain*, or did she know we were looking for her? Did she know she was waiting for me in a mass grave, that it wasn't her proper grave?
The *hoxha*, on deck, falls silent, *in harness*.

Your soul ought to have come across hers, in your dreams, the meeting point for encounters, that's what you were promised: while we are sleeping, our souls slip out of our bodies for a while to exchange experiences with other souls, living and dead, about the secret of dying. By practicing *going*

112

over, from life to death, from being to nothingness, our souls already know what is to be done when the body dies. We practice dying night after night, but I've never met Fahrie, you say, she didn't reveal any secrets to me, even though it's her duty to help me with dying.

Grief secures borrowed sisters for itself: a lump in your throat, stinging eyes, you cry unobtrusively, your face hardly contorted, as if you hadn't dried your glance well enough.

The grief broke in on tiptoe, picked all the locks without a skeleton key, not only making you believe it's outsize but maneuvering you into a corner: your thoughts and desires have moved to a spaceless dimension, driven out, like you they are the property of your tears, which hide in border zones, infecting, taking possession to the point of exhaustion. When you cry, it's difficult for me to keep my distance, to remain uninvolved; it frightens me to see you cry, even though I'm used to it.

Your grief ties you to Fahrie more than ever. It's a cul-de-sac, an *unconditional end*. You don't understand it, you can't bear not being able to comprehend it, you look for a way to get closer to it at all cost, ask the same questions again and again. The inevitability of it makes you sense that there's only one answer, since your boundaries are unalterable —
you renounce, you weep.

While you're weeping, you leave your body to its own devices, relinquish your unity with it; from now on, it will take over answering for you, you will only appear to be broken by the loss, in reality you will be taking leave: at the moment of mourning, you are saying farewell to yourself, and later on, when you're more familiar with mourning, you'll create a world in which the boundary between familiarity and strangeness will shift closer and closer to the former since only that can offer the security which makes a future possible —

if you cross that boundary, it's possible you might do something *inhuman.*
Do not be sorry.

We squat beside the grave, a strange growth.
The *hoxha* speaks, the *hoxha* sings, you weep, quietly as a little mouse. Fehmi speaks, Fehmi sings, you weep, quietly as a little mouse. The rest of the relatives speak and sing, one after the other, a collection of basses and baritones, you refuse, an unexpressed refusal in harmony with the repose of the afternoon, *surplus quiet*, in harmony with the silence, the language of the dead; when you fell silent, it was a capitulation in the face of the inevitable, less acceptance than an inability to react differently, lacking experience —
to understand, is it possible to understand death, which rejects any form of connection? Complete *aloneness*. Yet individuals are closer to the state of being dead: the Fahrie brand died out, Fahrie died out, not an everyday disaster but a misfortune that shoots out in all directions, everything has the task of failing (what could hurt more than to be forgotten as a lover, is it not your privilege as one of a pair of lovers to be unforgotten, that is to attain imaginary immortality? no, not a privilege, but your right as an imaginary immortal.)

After all, Fahrie can't even keep death as her sole possession. Her dying didn't belong to her, her death belongs to your family; from now on, she will just be your dead wife —
and what's all this about eternal love, *out of sight, out of mind*, you're already asking yourself whether you loved Fahrie or whether it was an illusion. She won't live on in you, she disqualified herself as a memory the moment she allowed herself to be abducted. Now the missing person has become the dead person —
So off to the wake, the funeral meats, pots and plates, bottles

114

and glasses. You stand apart, resisting the curse of the crippled mood and wait by the window for deliverance. But things haven't gotten that far yet, we're still in the middle of the prayers and you say:
Nothing is the way it should have been.

The way it should have been: a cool night, a new moon, a clear sky, a shooting star falls towards the earth. The next morning, Amra, the cockerel, crows like a cock and Fahrie, old, *old* Fahrie dies in her bed.
The *hoxha* is called and you hurry from house to house, the wailing, lamenting, singing starts up, you pray, *Godspeed to the world beyond, may you be welcomed there*, meanwhile the dead woman is undressed and washed.
With the body initially covered from the navel to the knees, your eldest daughter cleans it with a piece of cloth. She lifts the head slightly, cleans Fahrie's teeth and nostrils with two wet fingers, pours water over her trunk, rubs soap over it, first of all from the right, then from the left, dribbles perfume on her forehead, nose, hands, knees and feet, rubs it on her ear lobes, and carefully dries her mother with brief strokes and dabs; she folds the upper edge of the first shroud — there are three in all, they are white and smell of incense — over Fahrie's right side, the other edge over her left side, then wraps her in the same way in the second, finally in the third shroud. The face she leaves uncovered.
Your family come to see Fahrie for the last time, they say farewell to her by making a circular motion with their hands over her face, saying *God help you, God be with you*. Everyone sings, then you recite poems, tell stories, your mourning is demonstrative, as is right and proper. Tears stay within limits, only the women cry, the men hide their grief, they can only share it with their female relatives. They have to go and visit their sisters, *mourning journeys*, so that they can cry when their

brother-in-law is not at home; the women, on the other hand, only mourn in groups, a network on which the family can rely *at times of beginnings and ends*.

Then you empty all the water jugs and containers, for souls thirst after water and Fahrie's soul might abandon the funeral procession, jump into a forgotten can and drown: souls sink.

While the women stay at home guarding Fahrie's soul, it mustn't slip out of her body, you and your brother, brother-in-law, all your nephews and male friends are praying in the mosque, listening to the words of the *hoxha*, who talks at length about Fahrie, more than just impressions, he knew her well. Afterwards you carry the corpse in a procession to the graveyard, your women sing, things are simmering in the oven and the outsize gas urn is switched on to make *çaj*.

You dig until the hole is at least chest deep, your women roast, grill, and bake, you hollow out a recess in the grave, line it with a piece of cloth, your women lay out cutlery, plates, and cups, by yourself you lift Fahrie into her grave, turn her face towards Mecca, you say, *Dust we are, to dust we return, in the name of God and the belief in our prophet*, untie the knots at head and foot, throw three handfuls of earth on the body; before the women serve the food, you start to fill the grave and pray, *O our God, forgive this dead woman*.

Instead of all that, Fahrie's bones are lost in the coffin, knocking against the wood at every step, against *your ear*, a faint click, *sharp*.

The *hoxha* has ended the prayer. Your family line up side by side along the edge of the path, placing their right hands flat between heart and stomach. It's cramped for space around the graves, the mourners go in and out until they reach the path leading out, to Pristina. They say, *God be with you*, a wish delivered to each of the family as they pass —

to each one except you. You're still sitting by Fahrie's grave, uttering *telegrams from the end of the world:* no hell fire for her, you say, she won't have to drink hot water, won't be burnt up inside, boiled in the seven depths of hell, the immense funnel, not Fahrie, for her there's a place in the gardens of paradise with roads of red sapphire, yellow coral and white silver, four rivers in the countryside, flowing with milk and honey, water and wine, it's always sunny, never hot, pleasantly sunny with breezes rustling the leaves, shadows wandering from tree to tree, from soul to soul, wandering shadows, and Fahrie can eat and drink a hundred times more than on earth and she enjoys it a hundred times more.

Her house is in a village, similar to ours, richly furnished with velvet carpets, plush cushions, heavy sofas. Endless abundance: gold, silk, presents every day, journeys on the back of the birds of paradise, gliding between tongues of sunlight, sitting peacefully together under palm trees, never ending, in secluded ivy arbors, and Fahrie will never be ill again, never have to sleep again, will remain young forever, she'll lack for nothing.

When you eventually see her again, you'll recognize her immediately, for the soul borrows parts of the body, of the face —

I'd recognize her immediately, you say, and I'd be happy.

It's not right for you to show your devastation publicly; in the face of death, it's forbidden to express feelings, they could spread from face to face and from there penetrate more deeply, into bottomless depths.

Your relatives don't dare speak, don't dare move, they breathe very quietly, making sure their breath is hidden by the wind, the birds, the silence carves them in stone, fixes them to this one spot, a telephone sounds in the distance, playing its notes unceasingly; your grief is unseemly, repulsive, to watch you indecent.

They stand to one side, somewhat the worse for wear, waiting along the edges of the graveyard —
only a few new buildings, not yet finished, have managed to reach the vicinity, at first sight a flowery meadow, a refuge for butterflies, bumblebees, grasshoppers, bugs and spiders. Single plum trees, a thin copse of beeches on the western edge, poplars, oaks, and the tiled roofs of Pristina, thirsty roads in the distance. No footprints, they were churned up by vandals, rushes, creeping soft-grass, cornflowers, mallows, daisies, by copper queens with their broad noses and by thistles, a display of anonymous flowers, knee-deep, the earth uneven, one's right foot sinks in, the left one as well.

The gravestones too are nothing but white and black plants, petrified without stalks. They're at most twelve years old and not connected, either by paths or letters, no information as to how to find the dead. Just occasionally I find ones with a red double eagle and UÇK written on them. They have ageless faces on them, line drawings, the skin has the color of the stone. They're not portraits of the dead but illustrations, the illustration of Shaip Mushica, died 1999. How old is the man supposed to be, at what age does the engraving represent him? Was it done from a photograph, taken after his twentieth or fortieth birthday? The beard's deceptive, he was probably younger at the time, perhaps it was a bitterly cold winter, the sky black with flocks of crows, traces of fresh snow on the window ledge and the family huddled together to keep each other warm. Their lodging no more than a clean box, a greybeard of a room soaked with damp and mildew here and there, the cloth over the hearth singed, the only dry place; constantly wrestling with the cold, the family huddles together, there's *çaj*, *kafé*, security: a snapshot.
So much meadow, so little graveyard, falsifying history.

Back in the house we spread out over the third floor, there are things to eat and drink, the whole village is there, everyone who knew Fahrie. The mood, depressed, is just right, Emine takes me by the arm, explains *our customs*, never, never would they cremate someone, the body must be preserved, for *the life to come*. Graves, *huts for the dead*, were important, a person without a roof over their head was incredibly pitiful. During the burial as many steps as humanly possible must be taken; the more steps one took, the closer the deceased would come to heaven; and candles must burn for forty days, giving the deceased forty days to take their farewell, they came back while people were sleeping.

Against death: for forty days the dishes must not be washed in soapy water, for forty days voices must be no louder than a whisper; for forty days beards must not be shaved, clocks not wound up, *time stands still*. Only after forty days can we accept the death, Emine says, then we seek out a person who looks like the deceased from among our friends and relations, give them the deceased's clothes to put on, sit them in the vacated chair for a meal and they will talk to us, answer our questions as if they were the deceased. *Contact*, says Emine, in that way we feel the presence of the deceased, we're touched by their soul, at least for the duration of the meal.

Following that comes the excursion to the grave, a picnic with an accordion playing: in fact, this is the custom of her Serbian great-grandmother (on her father's side) who always smokes by the grave of her great-great-grandfather; she lights a cigarette for him as well, sticks it in the grave mound while the grandchildren and great-grandchildren are playing among the graves with no idea that they have come into contact with the souls of their ancestors. Great-grandmother smiles contentedly, fans herself and great-great-grandfather using yesterday's newspaper, the paper garden rustles and smells of printer's ink. Do you feel as hot as I do today? she whispers, waits a short while for his reply, then puts her bag over the shoulder, strokes her chin, and stamps her feet, getting herself ready for the walk home; unsteady on her feet, walking from one halt to the next, she will still go the other way home from the graveyard, the longer way, and she won't turn around, *more sensible than Orpheus.* That brings bad luck, she hisses, quickly hiding a bottle of plum brandy behind the gravestone.

Her house will stay open for seven days for people to come to offer their condolences, Emine says, but even after that, sometimes years later, the deceased will creep up on her in the form of a friend, an acquaintance, who has *only just* heard of her misfortune; baklava and tea in the reception room, polite condolences, sympathies. How can it be, *how can it be*, she'd thought she'd as good as gotten over the loss, and *every time*, every time she thinks she's managed to get rid of her grief, there's another knock at the door, *Sincere condolences*, and Emine wonders if they will ever let her go, the deceased —

so it's better to ignore the puzzle of the corpse, to neutralize the corpse, to make the departure from this life abstract.

Hot from walking, Sam leans into the breeze for a while, sways in the draft; to cut off his foreignness, leave it miles behind him, feel he belongs, live a normal life even in abnormal circumstances, *working on it in every wind that blows.*

As soon as he approaches, I recognize him from his footsteps, his staccato soles; an arm's length between us when he shakes my hand, hiccups in his eyes, I often find it difficult to believe, he says, that my work is helpful, brings something about. Private life is shipwrecked in the public sphere and sinks, *the world is simply bigger*, I wish we could rescue ourselves or be rescued by a ship's boat or a ship's passenger, I wish we could hold our own, I wish we had a chance against *collapses of time*, wars, natural catastrophes; love would be a sheet

anchor. His nod shuffles off his shoulder and, accompanied by the last red rays, he turns his back on the sun and closes his eyelids, just a little.
Talk to him.

You're leaning against the window, your face hidden in the curtain, your neck bent, the water on your cheeks beginning to dry, fine scratches on your hands —
such silence all around you that it seems futile to call you.
In that moment it becomes clear to me that we only encountered each other, nothing more —
this limitation creates freedom vis-à-vis me and you, the freedom not to have to assume any responsibility because assuming responsibility is beyond the bounds of possibility.

You're still waiting, apart, there was rage; half hidden behind cloth, you are both present and absent at the same time, being invisible it's not difficult —
you slip away in the darkness, your heart is pounding, you tie it tight and, battery driven as it seems to you, you take up position in the blind spot; an empty chair clatters uncomfortably in the hall, every groping movement a coat stand, your guitar, plump, a hiding place for a revolver, you feel your way around the corner, finally emerge in poor light; it's windy in the garden, branches scratching the fence, you order the escape car, unrecognized. At night the curves seem gentler, the roads shorter, the dim light of the street lamps makes distances deceptive, already the taxi's stopped, you pay, get out, go across the fields to her grave. Here it appears, *an ungrateful feeling* —
you think of Fahrie, in vain you try to call moments to mind and you dream of a meeting which never happened; you lean over the fence, the grave *playpen*, you lean over her grave to feel it, is it true, did it really happen, can you trust your hand,

121

the soil in your fingers? when you're startled by a voice, creeping up on your ear from behind, the voice of someone out for a nocturnal walk. Have you found what you lost? it asks.

9

Just a few days after the funeral you commit suicide. In my trouser pocket I find a piece of paper, directions to a place; I often get lost, too often, you got into the habit of drawing maps, just for me, the paths extra wide, the names extra large, a dot for my position, as if you always knew where I was to be found. Such confidence, admirable.

Acknowledgements:
I would like to thank Fadil Balia, Valerie Brasey (Office on Missing Persons and Forensics), Oran Finegan, Fatmire Shala (OMPF), James Nicholls (OMPF), Haxher Berani (OMPF), the Durmishi family, Prof. Karmit Zysman, Greta Kaçinari, Johanna Goldmann (Austrian Red Cross), Dr. Siroos Mirzaei (Hemayat Association), Dr. Barbara Preitler, Dragan Perak (Bosnian Cultural Center), Agron Bajrami, Tatjana Barislovic, Ilona Brzowski, Nikola Rupčič, Kristina Skrlin and all those whom I can/may not mention by name, for all the long conversations, their detailed answers to my questions, their explanations, discussions, support, patience, and time.

The Translator:
For many years a lecturer in German at Stirling University with a special interest in Austrian literature, Michael Mitchell has been a full-time literary translator since 1995 and has published some sixty books in translation from German and French, ranging from classics (Grimmelshausen, Goethe, Adolf Loos, Oskar Kokoschka, Georges Rodenbach) to contemporary writers (Helmut Krausser, Josef Winkler, Werner Schwab, Frank Schätzing). He has been shortlisted for prizes on numerous occasions and he was awarded the 1998 Schlegel-Tieck Prize for Herbert Rosendorfer's *Letters Back to Ancient China.*